Franklin P. Rice, John S. C. Knowlton, Clarendon Wheelock

Carl's Tour in Main Street

Franklin P. Rice, John S. C. Knowlton, Clarendon Wheelock

Carl's Tour in Main Street

ISBN/EAN: 9783337191733

Printed in Europe, USA, Canada, Australia, Japan

Cover: Foto ©Andreas Hilbeck / pixelio.de

More available books at **www.hansebooks.com**

WORCESTER MASS
SANFORD AND PA
MDCCCLXXXIX

NOTE.

"CARL'S TOUR IN MAIN STREET" was the joint production of John S. C. Knowlton and Clarendon Wheelock. The latter, familiar from early life with Worcester men, localities and affairs, supplied the incidents from his store of recollection; and Mr. Knowlton rendered them into the charming and quaintly-phrased story, imparting to it the quality and interest of a veritable narrative. The "Tour" was published in numbers in the *Worcester Palladium* (of which Mr. Knowlton was the founder, and until his death, the editor) of 1855: and was by request reprinted in that paper in 1857–58, and again in 1874.

In preparing this fourth edition of "Carl's Tour" for the types, I have corrected some obvious errors, and have added a few references for the benefit of those who are not familiar with time's changes in Worcester. Although the statements made are not always in strict accordance with historical accuracy, I have thought it best not to change the narrative in any essential particular; nor have I availed myself of the privilege to add notes to an extent that would encumber the text, most of which is self-explanatory.

The frontispiece engraving represents a view of the north entrance to the village of Worcester in 1839, from Lincoln street, looking west and south over Lincoln square. It is enlarged from a drawing made by J. W. Barber, and printed in his "Historical Collections of Massachusetts."

FRANKLIN P. RICE.

May, 1889.

CHAPTER I.

Mr. Editor: I never go far from home; but I remember that about twenty years ago I made a tour through our Main street. It was a bright autumnal day, in the good month of October, when my venerable father —peace to his ashes, and forever green be his memory —took down his hat from the peg on which it was his custom to hang it, and said to me: "Come, Carl, let us go to the Common, and see the Cattle Show." In less than six minutes I was six inches taller; and washing my face, as all travellers should when setting out on a long journey, and taking down my cap from the peg on which it hung, below my father's, I put it on my head, and we sallied forth, hand in hand, to witness a Worcester County *Carnival.*

Our house was not far from Lincoln Square. At that time the Square retained, more than it now does,

the character it once had as the centre of trade, of
fashion, and of life in our then quiet country village.
There were five roads that then led out of the Square.
One of them was Lincoln street, which was then, as
it long had been, the great travelled road to Boston,
and over which run daily innumerable stages, and
baggage wagons, and pleasure carriages, making their
way between the metropolis, the Connecticut valley,
and the country beyond.   It was the old mail road,
on which the mails used, in the olden time, as my
father informed me, to be carried from Boston to
Philadelphia, and back in three weeks.   It was on
Lincoln street, he also told me—and he pointed out
the place—where the Hancock Arms Tavern stood;
nearly opposite where the Gas Works now are.   It
was the resort, in olden times of the wits and wags and
merry topers of the "north end;" and the headquarters of the army of insurgents in the Shays rebellion.
It had probably outlived its day, and been supplanted
by a more modern rival; for my father informed me
that after standing unoccupied for several years, it was
fired by an incendiary, and burned to the ground some
ten years before I first attended cattle show.

There were but few houses on Lincoln street at the

time my memory of things begins, and none of the streets in existence that now lead out of it at right angles. It was lined on both sides, mainly, by the splendid farm of Gov. Lincoln, senior; and his mansion house stood a quarter of a mile out of the Square, on the west side of the street. The grounds about it were the finest in Worcester. Attached to it was a splendid garden; and in the rear a beautiful pond, which the hand of improvement has sadly marred in these later days; and in front was the fine farm, extending half a mile to the east. Mr. Lincoln was a man of mark in the country. He filled the office of attorney general of the United States in Jefferson's cabinet, and lived and died a democrat. Although his house was a fine one in his day, and as well supplied as any in the country, yet he never had but one room carpeted: painted board floors being thought good enough in those times for the best of people. I was pained, a few years ago, to see that house shoved off its foundations, to make room for the more palace-like dwelling of an enterprising and wealthy mechanic. It stands now on the corner of Grove and Lexington streets. The Lincoln grounds are no longer the farm they were when I used to run over them in my boyhood.

Streets have been cut through them ; trees have fallen before the axe ; and a railroad has usurped one side of the pond, and robbed it of the quietude that once made its banks a charming sylvan retreat.

Higher up Lincoln street, and north of the Lincoln mansion, was the fine old country seat of the Paine family. My father told me that it had never changed within his knowledge. It was Timothy Paine, if I remember rightly, that first planted himself there. He held various public offices, and before the Revolution he was appointed a Councillor to the royal governor. The people took a more patriotic view of the matter than he did, gathered around his house in great numbers, and thus induced him to relinquish the appointment. My father said that he never knew Esq. Paine : but that he knew his son, Dr. William Paine, who opened the first apothecary shop in Worcester ; that he was in England purchasing goods when the war broke out, and for some reason, which I do not now remember, he did not return home, but joined the British army in the capacity of a surgeon. After the war was over, however, he returned home, and in some way regained posession of his confiscated estate, which has been in the Paine family ever since,—a part of which is the splendid hill, now covered with wood, which lies east of the house, and will one day be a fortune of itself.

On our way to the Cattle Show, my father pointed out the spot where the first saw and grist mill was built by the first settlers in Worcester. It was back of the residence of the late Madame Salisbury, near where stands the freight depot of the Nashua railroad. A dam was there thrown across Bimeleck, or Fort River, as Mill Brook was then called; the water setting back and covering the low ground far up the stream, and coming, my father said, quite up to the travelled way of Lincoln street. He said that he had heard that there was a garrison near by, to defend the mills from attack by the Indians; but he was not certain of the truth of it.

At the time of which I am speaking, another road came into the Square from the east. It was then a turnpike, running from Worcester to Boston, straight over hills and valleys, rivers and ponds, and turning neither to the right nor the left. It ran over the north wing of Chandler hill, and by the side of Bladder Pond; and now bears the more fanciful name of Belmont street.

Salisbury street—the old road to Holden—led out of the Square in a northwest direction ; and Main street and Summer street in a southerly direction, diverging as they extended. Union and Highland streets were not laid out. Grove, Concord, Lexington, Prescott and Otis streets were then a cow pasture. The beautiful sheet of water, now known as Salisbury Pond, had no existence twenty years ago. The land it covers was then a meadow, with a brook meandering through it, over which I have crossed many a time, in my play, on a rail, where the water is now the deepest. The dam, which is now a part of Grove street, had not then been built ; and I desire here to thank the city government of the last year for the erection of a substantial sidewalk of timber and plank, on the edge of the dam, which adds so much to the convenience and comfort of the thousands, who, in pleasant weather,—especially on Sunday afternoons—walk through Grove street, to visit our beautiful Rural Cemetery, where so many of the friends of the present generation of the residents of Worcester rest from life's turmoils, and where they will one day be joined by those they have left behind.

Yours, ever,

CARL.

CHAPTER II.

Mr. Editor: In speaking of Lincoln street in my last letter, I forgot to mention that my father told me, when we were on our way to the Cattle Show, that there was once a Scotch Church in Worcester. It consisted, he said, of a little colony of Scotchmen, who came over early, and located themselves around the head waters of Bimeleck. They were an industrious and frugal people, who, if let alone, would have been a valuable addition to the settlement: for it was the Scots, my father said, who first cultivated the potatoe in New England: spun flax with the foot wheel, and wove it into linen cloth, and showed themselves adepts in other useful arts. But there was a prejudice against them, which lost no opportunity to give itself an airing. Having their own religious opinions and attachments, the Scotch settlers in Worcester desired to worship by themselves; and they, therefore, under-took the erection, for themselves, of a meeting house. My father pointed out, as near as he was able, the spot where they raised the frame of a wooden church. My recollection of the place is not very distinct at this day; but it was near the top of the hill in Lincoln street,—a little north of the Paine house, and in a position to command a pleasant prospect of the sur-rounding country. I regret for the reputation of the " rude forefathers of the hamlet," that the frugal and pious Scotchmen were not allowed to enjoy their free-dom of conscience without molestation. But such was not the case. My father told me that before the Scotch meeting house was completed, the rest of the people in the settlement rose in a body—respectable gentlemen and all—went to the church, under cover of the darkness of night, and razed the building to the ground, not leaving one stick upon another. The poor Scotch settlers " pulled up stakes," and found homes in other localities.

It was about twenty years ago, you will remember, that I told you my father said to me, one pleasant October day: " Come, Carl, let us go and see the Cattle Show," and that he took down his hat—it was a broad-brim—and I my cap, from the pegs on which it was our custom to hang them ; and we sallied forth on our tour through Main street, from the North end to the South end.   At that time, as I said before, there were five roads—there are seven now—running out of Lincoln Square, which lies at the North end of Main street, and across which runs the ancient Bimeleck— the modern Mill Brook—under a stone arch bridge, as wide as the Square is wide.   In my boy days, it was my custom to admire that bridge, it was so roomy, and nothing pleased me more than to see the stage-men drive their teams into the water at the North end, and wash their coaches and refresh their horses, after finishing their trip for the day from Boston on the east, or Springfield, or Northampton, or Hartford on the west.   It seemed to my boy eyes, that the coach-man who held the reins and cracked the whip for a team of four, was the most exalted man in the nation. Certain it is that I always made my bow to the coach-man, instead of those who rode behind him.   There was music in his post-horn, which the steam whistle does not begin to rival.

At the time I went through Lincoln Square, on my way with my father to the Cattle Show, its appearance

was very different from what it now is. The Salisbury
mansion stood then as it now stands, except that
shortly afterwards I was astonished one day to see the
workmen put screws under it, and give it an elevation
of some half a dozen feet from the ground more than
it had before.   On the opposite side of the brook,
where stands now the passenger station house of the
Worcester and Nashua railroad, stood at that time, and
for years afterwards, a one-story wooden building,
which, my father told me, was the store in which the
elder Mr. Salisbury carried on, for a long time, an
extensive trade with Worcester and the country around,
keeping, as was the custom of the time, a supply
of West India and dry goods, and laying the foundation
of that ample fortune which makes, at this day, the
Salisbury estate one of the richest in the country, out
of the large cities.   I can but think, however, that
something of success in this instance was owing to
the habits of economy and frugality, which marked
the early life of that gentleman ; and which it would
be better for the young men of to-day, who are in business, if they would study and imitate.   My father said
he knew him well, that he was always behind his
counter, or in his little counting room, giving the

most scrupulous attention to every matter of business, no matter how inconsiderable, and retiring at night to a small room connected with his store, where he slept as the guard of his own property. Some one has kept a record of the young men who have commenced life as dealers in dry goods, and shows the failure of 95 in every 100. Is it not to be attributed, in a great degree, to an extravagance in the way of doing business, and of living, which did not prevail with those who were the business men of half a century ago?

My father pointed out to me the place where the elder Daniel Waldo—father of the late Daniel Waldo —kept store in the revolutionary times, but it has gone from my memory. I remember that he said that Mr. Waldo owned the first chaise that run in Worcester and that as he came originally from Boston, and was so extravagant as to ride in a chaise, his neighbors looked upon him as somewhat of an aristocrat. He told me also, an anecdote of what a narrow escape that gentleman run in the time of the Shays rebellion. It was cold and blustering weather, the Shays men were quartered at the Hancock Arms hotel, where the alarm was given that many of the soldiers had been poisoned by some unseen hand : that many were sick, and perhaps all of them would die. The surgeon of the regiment made an examination, and discovered that some deadly drug had been mingled with the sugar which the soldiers used, to sweeten their toddy. It was ascertained that the sugar had been bought at Mr. Waldo's store, and as he was not in favor of the rebellion, it was believed that he had purposely put poison into the sugar to destroy the rebellionists. An officer with a file of soldiers was sent to arrest the offender. They marched him to the Hancock Arms, where it was proposed to subject him to what is now denominated Lynch law. But execution was delayed until some one or more soldiers should die of the poison. In the mean time the discovery was made that the poisonous substance in the toddy was nothing but yellow snuff, which by some accident had been dropped into the sugar, and the offender was discharged upon the payment of a fine of a barrel of rum.

Twenty years ago, when I set out on my travels, what is now the Nashua Hotel was a two-story public house, standing several rods east of its present location. It has since been moved, and modernized and renovated, I hope, in more ways than one. It was a good inn for the accommodation of *beasts*, but a terrific place for *men*. It was a "rum tavern" in its most fiery signification. It had a long piazza in front, and there sat the *signs*, from morning to night, of the business carried on within ; a blotched and bloated row of frail mortality, the sight of which always made the marrow creep in my bones whenever I had occasion to run by it. Some of those poor unfortunates I knew by sight. The sods of the valley now press upon their lips ; or, I doubt not, they would speak, with terrible earnestness, to every young man, the burning words, " *Touch not the drunkard's cup!*"

> " It weaves the winding sheet of souls,
> And lays them in the urn of everlasting sleep."

In this connection, I am reminded of a man by the name of *Pete Johnson*, who, I doubt not, is remembered by many of your city readers. Years ago, Pete kept a rum shop on the east side of Lincoln Square, in the basement of the brick building now occupied by the Washington Engine Company,—and a first-rate fire company it is too. I used to be pleased to hear the fire bells, for, boy as I was, I was sure to steal away from home and "run" with that company to

fires.   There was in it an excitement that was almost
fun.   Pete was a great talker, and a great wag.   I
believe he was a native of Worcester; but I know not
what became of him.   He had always his story to tell,
and I would go without my dinner any time for the
sake of listening to one of Pete's stories.   Temperance
and temperance men were never favorites with him.
One of his stories was this (though I am aware that I
cannot tell it with any of the grace with which he told
it): "When they were building the Western Railroad to Albany (said he) I went up into York state,
and hired a small tavern, at no great distance from a
hard-work in the track.   I kept the house solely for
the accommodation of *travellers*, you know.   Yet I
was very much annoyed by the Irish workmen upon
the railroad coming to get rum to drink.   It worried
me to see them waste their money so; but yet as they
would waste it, I thought I might as well have it as
somebody else.   And as I was anxious for their good,
I hit upon a plan, which was alike beneficial to them
and to me.   They would come to my house so drunk
that I did not dare refuse them what they called for;
and as they called for drink after drink, *I put in more*

and more water, until, in the end, they had drunk so much water that they went away quite sober." Pete was a philosopher in dram drinking, and at the same time had an eye to the improvement of his finances.

Yours,

CARL.

CHAPTER III.

Mr. Editor: At the close of my last letter we had made our entrance into Lincoln Square on our way to Main street. Crowds of people were passing along in the same direction. My father told me to note them well, and see how great was the diversity of character and conduct, " for (said he) it is such a crowd as you will see no other day in the year, whatever may be the holiday." I did observe the crowd, and I have not failed to obey the injunction every year since. There were old men and young men, striplings and boys, old ladies and young ladies, misses and girls ; many riding and many walking, high crown and low crown, broad brim and narrow brim, long waist and short waist, the modest cottage head gear and the flaunting flare up, the long skirt and the short skirt, the poor and the rich, the substantial yeoman, and the

vulgar cockney, and last, though not least, a caravan
of pedlers, all going to see and enjoy the Farmer's
Annual Holiday ; and perhaps with no higher ambi-
tion in many of them, than honestly, or dishonestly, to
" turn a penny."

I was on tiptoe with the multitude to see the sights,
but when we got into the Square, my father chilled
me with the remark, " Come, Carl, go with me into
the jail.   I must see my old friend M."   "Why, what
is he there for?   What has he been doing, that they
shut him up?   Is he a rogue?"   Such were the questions that I put in quick succession.   "No (was the
answer), he has only been unfortunate.   He owes
money which he cannot pay."   In my simplicity I
asked the question, " And how can he pay it by being
in prison?"   It's the law," was the ready reply.

We called at the tavern, kept by Mr. Bellows.   It
stood on the south side of the Square, at the corner of
Summer street, where now stands the large brick
building that was erected for the accommodation of
the Worcester Branch Railroad.   The house was
crowded with people ; there was no Maine law in
those days ; but my father found the turnkey, and we
went to the jail.   It was a large stone building, which

2

stood a little way from the house, near where Union street now enters the Square. Massive iron doors were opened one after another, with huge keys, and we climbed up stone steps after stone steps until we reached the third story. "Those rooms below (said my father), are for the criminals, these for the poor debtors." Another lock was turned, the iron door creaked on its hinges, we were ushered into M's cell, and the door shut and locked upon us. "Come in half an hour," said my father to the turnkey; and this was my first half hour in prison. I have been in jails, and houses of correction, and state prisons, since that time, but never with such emotions as moved my inmost heart on that occasion.

Mr. M. (and his image haunts me) was a man of middle age, and of middling stature. He gave my father a cordial welcome. He looked pensive. For furniture there was a small bed on one side of the cell, two chairs, and a small unpainted table, on which were two or three books and a newspaper. "I was looking over my book of accounts (said he) as you entered, to see if there is anything to prevent my taking the oath. I could pay all my debts if men would pay me what they owe me; but if they will not, or can not, then I must suffer the consequences." I was then taking my first lesson in the philosophy of the relation of debtor and creditor, and have since found it a circular chain, the links of which are all dependent upon each other. They talked fast. My father was more cheerful in jail than out. M. smiled occasionally a sardonic smile, and I busied myself in looking out, as well as I could, at the grated window, and in examining every nook and crevice, scratch and mark, upon the forbidding walls and dirty ceiling. The turnkey came back and opened the door. I started out. Mr. M. patted me on my head, and made some remark which I do not now remember; and as I looked back I saw my father take something from his pocket and give to him; but what it was I did not see, and he would not tell me, though I often asked him the question.

When we passed down stairs, and had reached the lower floor, my father halted for a moment at the door of a cold and dreary cell. "This (said he), was for many years the miserable cell of the howling, naked, filthy maniac, Peter Sibley, of Sutton, who was tried for murder, and acquitted by the jury on the ground of insanity. The boys would come under his window to ' stir him up,' as they said, that they might hear his insane ravings. It was for him, and such as he, that the State built its Lunatic Hospitals ; and he has been taken out and carried there." Years afterwards, when I came to understand the subject better, I saw, in one of the wards of the hospital, the " howling, naked, filthy maniac," transformed into the quiet, neat, and well-dressed patient, whom no one would mistrust for an insane man, were it not for the expression of the countenance, which is as plainly the language of insanity, to one who can read it, as though it were written in letters and words upon the pallid brow. Sibley lived incurably insane, and died but a little while ago, having been in confinement well nigh forty years.

When we had reached the street in front of the jail my father turned round and surveyed it with his eye, letting fall some remark about the " progress of civilization," which I did not fully hear nor comprehend. " Your grandfather told me (said he), that when the county was incorporated, about a hundred years ago (it was in 1731), they built a cage in the back part of the Jennison house, just south of the Unitarian meeting house ; but that in the course of a few months they moved the cage to the house of Mr. Daniel Heywood, where now stands the new City Hall.* A jail was built, as soon it could be done conveniently, north of the Square, which lasted about twenty years, when a larger one was built near by, and after about thirty years more this one was erected." He said that he remembered well when it was built; that it was one of the first buildings of stone erected in the commonwealth, and drew from every one the remark that "it would last and serve the county for hundreds of years." In less than half a century it had been leveled with the ground, as unsuited to the wants of a growing community, and not one stone was left upon another. The little "rum tavern" took its departure about the same time, and on the spot where it stood the enterprising firm of Joseph Walker & Sons† now manufacture, daily, hundreds of pairs of boots, without the help of the "evil spirits," or the toddy stick, that danced attendance on their revels. A railroad now occupies the ground between where once stood the inn and the jail, and over it run hourly, trains of cars that never entered into the dreams of the thousands of

*Now Bay State House.

†Now Dean Building (?).

"poor debtors," whose limited occupation it had been to look out through the grates, and gaze, in vain regrets, upon a patch, here and there, of blue sky.

"I pity him, poor fellow (said my father, as he stood looking up to the grated window) but I cannot help him." "Why can you not help him?" inquired I with innocent simplicity. "Because, my son, I have no money to spare. It takes all I can get to—— (I lost the rest of the sentence) and I must be just before I can be generous. I must try and keep out of debt, or I may have to go to jail myself, and you will then come and pity me in my cell, as you have now pitied Mr. M."

We started along towards Main street. Between the jail and Mill Brook stood a two-story wooden building, on the lower floor of which our present worthy Register of Probate* had his law office, and over it was a small tenement, which was reached by a flight of stairs out of doors, standing within a few feet of the water. We had just entered upon the bridge, when I heard the door of that house open, and looking round, over my left shoulder, I saw a [man stagger out of the door, and pitch head foremost from

*Charles G. Prentiss, Esq.

the top to the bottom of the stairs. "Oh. the poor drunkard," said my father, "that's the end of him." We turned about and walked quickly to the spot. His wife came running down the stairs. We lifted him up, expecting his neck was broken, or the breath beat out of his body, when he opened his eyes with an unearthly stare, and exclaimed, "Let me alone, I know what I 'm about, I 've been to Cattle Show once, and I'm going again, so hands off!" His grief-stricken wife looked up as if oppressed with the consciousness that this world had no holiday for her, and with the remark, "I'll take care of him," she thanked us for our kindness, and we turned away.

Yours, ever,

CARL.

CHAPTER IV.

Mr. Editor : — As we walked away from the jail, and crossed the bridge at Lincoln Square, my father remarked ; " This is not now the ' Bridge of Sighs,' though I think it might have been in the olden time." I inquired what he meant ; and he said there was once a " love affair near by, which made much talk in the time of it."

He said that among the Scotch settlers in Worcester, there came over an Irish family by the name of Rankin. They had several daughters, the youngest of whom was Anna. At that time there was a family here, very respectable for the times, by the name of Andrews. One of the boys was named Samuel, who was at the time an undergraduate in Harvard College. Sam. came home to spend a vacation, and while at home he saw Anna Rankin ; and taking a liking to

" her neck," which, like Kathleen Bawn's was " so soft, and so smooth, without freckle or speck," he " fell in love," as the novel-writers say. He forthwith threw Latin and Greek to the dogs; made love to Anna, and in due time married her; and, purchasing a farm down on the west side of Quinsigamond Lake, he settled down and became an industrious and frugal yeoman. In that occupation he prospered so well that in a few years he quitted his farm, and moved into the village, and built him a house on the very spot where the stone jail was subsequently erected. Afterwards he built him a larger and better house on ground now occupied by the block of brick houses opposite the court house. Father and mother both died, leaving an only daughter, named Anna, after her mother, with an estate that made her the principal heiress of Worcester in those times.

In the rear of the Andrews house, Tim. Bigelow had a blacksmith's shop, where he blew the bellows, heated and hammered the iron, shod the horses and oxen, and mended the ploughs and chains for the farmers of the country about him. Now Tim. was as " bright as a button," more than six feet high; straight and handsome, and walked upon the earth with a natural air and grace that was quite captivating.

Tim. saw Anna and Anna saw Tim. and they were well satisfied with each other.   But as he was then " nothing but Tim. Bigelow, the blacksmith," the lady's friends, whose ward she was, would not give their consent to a marriage.   So, watching an opportunity, the lovers mounted fleet horses and rode a hundred miles to Hampton, in New Hampshire, which lies on the coast between Newburyport and Portsmouth, and was at that time the "Gretna Green" for all young men and maidens for whom "true love" did not "run a smooth course" in Massachusetts. They came back to Worcester as Mr. and Mrs. Timothy Bigelow.   He was a man of decided talent, and well fitted by nature for a popular leader.   All the leading men of the town at that time were tories. He espoused the cause of the people, and soon had a party strong enough to control the town ;   and being known as a patriot, he was soon recognized by Hancock, Samuel Adams, Gen. Warren, James Otis, and others of the patriot party throughout the Province. He was sent as a delegate from Worcester to the provincial congress ;   and as captain of the Minute Men he led his company from Worcester to Cambridge, on the 19th of April, 1775, at the summons of a messenger who rode swiftly into town that day, on a large white horse, announcing that the war had begun. For a long time afterwards, (my father told me,) that express man was always spoken of as "death on a pale horse."

If your readers will consult a history of the Revolutionary War, they will find that the blacksmith Bigelow soon rose to the rank of Major, and afterwards to that of Colonel of the 15th Massachusetts regiment, which was composed almost exclusively of Worcester county men; that he was at the storming of Quebec; at the taking of Burgoyne; in the terrific scenes of Valley Forge; and on almost every other field made memorable by the fierce conflicts of the revolution. When the war was over he returned home, his constitution shattered by hard service for his country; his occupation gone; his money matters in sad derangement, in consequence of that formidable depreciation of the currency, under which forty dollars was scarcely sufficient to pay for a pair of shoes; and he died at what was long known as the "Bigelow Mansion"—formerly the Andrews house— about 65 years ago, and just after he had passed the 50th year of his life. And thus ended the "love affair," which, my father said, produced a prodigious excitement in its day.

A son of Col. Bigelow bore the name of his father, and was for a long time a prominent lawyer at Groton and afterwards at Medford in Middlesex county. He was repeatedly elected a representative and senator in the general court; was one of the governor's council; ten times speaker of the house; and was also a member of the famous Hartford convention. He was one of the wittiest men of his time; and as a specimen of his wit, my father told me that he stepped into the house of representatives one day when Mr. Bigelow was in the chair. A clumsy member undertook to walk across the area in front of the speaker's desk, made a blunder, and fell at full length on the floor. A shout of laughter followed, in which all the members seemed to participate. Speaker Bigelow sprung upon his feet in an instant, and exclaimed in a loud voice: — "Order, gentlemen! Mr. —— *has the floor!*"

John P. Bigelow, formerly secretary of state, and recently mayor of the city of Boston, was a son — and Mrs. Abbott Lawrence, a daughter, of the second Timothy Bigelow; and I am thinking that they have no occasion to be ashamed of their descent from the poor Irish emigrant girl, Anna Rankin.

Thus as by an irresistible destiny, runs on the

chain of life's changes; linking on generation after generation, and binding together the last and the first of the human race.   In this instance I have followed it through six generations.   First, there was the humble emigrant with the Scotch Presbyterians, James Rankin.   Second, his daughter Anna, who married young Samuel Andrews.   Third, their daughter Anna Andrews, the heiress, who eloped with Tim. Bigelow, whose blacksmith's shop stood where the Court Mills now stand, and who figured so largely in the Revolution.   Fourth, Timothy Bigelow, the younger, the lawyer and the statesman.   Fifth, the ex-mayor; and the wife of the millionaire who recently represented the United States at the court of St. James.   And sixth, the sons and the daughters, who if not already known to fame, may be hereafter.   I wish I knew as well the history of all the early settlers in Worcester.   It would give me pleasure to jot it down.   But perhaps the remark of my father about the "love affair" gave me an interest in this piece of family history greater than I could feel in any other. We are rarely masters of our own will.

Yours truly,

CARL.

CHAPTER V.

Mr. Editor : — I fear that some of your readers may be afflicted with the idea that they may not live long enough to see *the other end* of my tour. If so, let me remind them that Rome was not built in a day; that the siege of Troy lasted ten years; and that all great undertakings require time — much time.

The Antiquarian Hall was an object of interest, twenty years ago, to every visitor in Lincoln Square; especially if he had a taste for the elevated pleasures and refinements of life, and could see something to live for more ennobling than the mere *getting of money.* The Hall was built about thirty-five years ago by the notable Isaiah Thomas. In the course of a long life, devoted to the printing and publishing of books, he had accumulated a great variety of books, pamphlets, newspapers, etc., ; and he conceived the

idea of an institution that might be of great utility as
a depository of the facts of past times, and the material
for the future to illustrate American history. He
founded the American Antiquarian Society; gave to
it all his valuable collections; and built the Hall, and
gave it, with the land which it occupied, to the
Society. A few years afterwards, as my father
informed me, the Society found itself so well prospered
that it was obliged to enlarge its accommodations by
adding wings to the main building. The location
of the building was found in time not to be a good
one for the preservation of books; and the Society has
built a new Hall on the west side of the Square; and
the old hall is now temporarily occupied by the
Worcester Academy, since the sale of its lands and
buildings as too valuable to be occupied for educational purposes.

In my boy days it was always a pleasure to me to
stroll into the Antiquarian Hall; to see its alcoves
well lined with books, though I could not conceive it
possible that any one could ever think of reading
them; to look by the hour at the multitude of little
portraits that hung in the gallery; and to see the
Indian relics and other antiquities, and especially that

modern antique the leviathan Jewsharp, which was presented to some odd fellows in Worcester by some merry wags on the Kennebec. But the chief pleasure of my visits always was to see the librarian himself; who could be man or boy at a moment's warning; was always on a level with either; had ever something to say that it was a pleasure to me to listen to; and abounded with humor that oozed out even at his fingers' ends. Fond as I then was of *new* books, I could not understand his passion for *old* ones, and I never left him without receiving his paternal blessing, and a most importunate injunction : — " If you find any *old books*, bring them to me ! "

I remember an incident. I was at play in the Square one pleasant summer afternoon when there drove into the capacious yard of the Lincoln Square Hotel — in front of the house — a man in a wagon, who was carrying an ass to market. He loosed the horse from the wagon, and put him in the stable to feed, leaving the ass standing up on all fours in the wagon. I had never seen an ass before, and I walked about and surveyed him at every point. Presently I saw the librarian and another gentleman, smaller than he was, come out of the Hall, and walk rapidly

towards the wagon.   As they came up they both burst
into a loud laugh.   They walked around the wagon
time and again, and looked at the animal before and
behind, and the more they walked and looked the
more they laughed.

"Christopher," said the small man, " I'm going to
speak to him ! "

" That's right, William," said the librarian, " but
I don't believe he will condescend to make you any
answer ! "

Taking off his hat, and making a low bow to the
ass, the man of small stature said to him in the most
respectful manner :

" How does your majesty?   If there is anything
in the power of your humble servant to do for the
comfort of your majesty, your majesty will please
to command his most ready service."

No answer.

" Perhaps," said William, " I have mistaken your
character.   Although your ass-ship looks very much
like a king, it is possible, after all, that your reverence
is the more respectable personage of a professional
gentleman ; a reverend doctor of divinity, on your
way to exchange pulpits with some brother ; a presi-

3

dent or professor of a college, making a tour in a college vacation ; or possibly a judge, riding his circuit. What, not a word in reply ? Then I am most grievously disappointed and mortified, that your honor will not condescend to speak to so humble an individual as he who now addresses you. You try him, Christopher ! "

" That I will," said the librarian, walking up to the ass and holding out his hand. "How do you do, brother — *John Tail?*"

" He, he, ha, ha ! " went William ; " I should think you would feel mortified yourself now, Christopher, to find that the ass does not condescend to know *his own brother* before folks."

" Brother ass ! " said the librarian, " we see that you are 'up in the world,' and we rejoice in your prosperity. Perhaps you are on your way to Boston, to take a seat in the legislature ; or to Washington to become a member of congress, or president. If so, do not look with such indifference upon your lowly and less fortunate brothers."

No response from the ass.

" You try him now, my young man," said the librarian to me, " and see if you can draw from him a specimen of his vocabulary."

I walked up to the ass's head, patted his neck gently, rubbed lightly his furry ears and his velvet nose, and slipping my hand into my pocket I drew therefrom a cake of gingerbread, which the animal took and devoured with avidity. " If you want some more, say so," said I to the ass. And thereupon he opened his mouth, and let out one of his loudest brays. It was as fiercely loud as the screeching of the hoarsest steam whistle, and almost as sonorous as the crowing of a Shanghai cockerel. It seemed as though the librarian and his friend would have died in an ecstasy of humor at the exhibition. They patted the ass, and they patted me. They walked backward and forward, and laughed and held their sides, until the poor ass seemed to be almost conscious that he had provoked all their mirth.

It was not very long after this life-scene in Lincoln Square that I was pained one day to hear my father read in a newspaper that the librarian was thrown from the top of a stage coach, when travelling in Ohio, and instantly killed. His humorous, talented and highly intellectual friend survived him many years; but his brimming cup of genial humor had become to some extent embittered by those in whom he had too generously confided.

The new Antiquarian Hall has been the subject of sharp criticism. It certainly has an odd exterior; but I am not connoisseur enough to decide whether it violates the rules of architectural propriety. Its interior is very handsome and convenient; and I am charitable enough to the Society to entertain the belief that it suffers more from its location than from any fault in its architectural design. Its site is too elevated above the surrounding grounds. It would look far better if it stood upon a plain, embowered with trees and shrubbery. As it is, one looks at it now as a lover upon his knees looks in the face of his mistress; and though I never served on a nunnery committee, I think you will not get so good a view of the lady's countenance when looking up at an angle of forty-five degrees as you do when looking her horizontally in the face. The site is in many respects a fine one. It is elevated, airy and accessible; and resting upon a ledge of rocks it is beyond the reach of moisture, so injurious to books. Twenty years ago there stood upon the spot a small wooden house, even then ancient in appearance, which was occupied by Mr. Peter Williams, who had been then, my father told me, for a long time an attaché of the Salisbury estate.

Venerable with age, he is, I think, still in that service.

At the time I commenced my tour through Main street, there was a wooden building standing at the southwest corner of Lincoln Square, about where the bank wall now terminates in front of the court houses. It was then a grocery; but my father said that it had been noted for many years in his day as the headquarters of the democratic politicians of Worcester. Dr. Abraham Lincoln, he said, kept an apothecary shop there, and there the politics of the day were discussed. My father said that Dr. Lincoln loved politics and segars equally well; and all day long he would sit with his heels up, smoking his much loved "Indian weed." The doctor's wife, my father told me, was the eldest daughter of Col. Timothy Bigelow, the blacksmith officer. Besides being chosen to town offices, the doctor was elected a member of the constitutional convention of 1820; also to the general court, and to the executive council, of which he was a member at the time of his death; and as that was before my day I think he must have died at least thirty years ago.

Yours,

CARL.

CHAPTER VI.

Mr. Editor.—Twenty years ago the brick Court House was the most attractive building in Worcester. As I lived in its vicinity, it was always the great pleasure of my boy days when there was no school, to get the privilege of my father to go into the court house, and hear the trials. "You can learn what mischief and crime is," said my father; "and when you see how rogues are punished, I hope you will learn not to be a rogue yourself." I remembered my father's remark; and I think I profited by the scenes I often witnessed. I was touched once, I remember, by the trial of a small boy. He had stolen a few dollars in money from the man with whom he lived. On the trial he had no one to speak for him; and for that reason, I suppose, he received a hard sentence. To my limited vision the judges then appeared to me the biggest men in the universe. The Hon. Calvin Willard, now living in well-deserved retirement, then filled the chair of high sheriff, and represented, in his bearing in court, the dignity and honor of the commonwealth. Silas Brooks performed serious service for the court, by uttering the short but expressive prayer, every morning, noon and night: — "*God save the Commonwealth of Massachusetts!*" Hon. Abijah Bigelow filled the place of clerk ; and, with a voice peculiarly his own, he put the jurors upon the panel, and administered the oath. I supposed the voice was one that belonged to the office, and not to the man ; and I was not undeceived until the late Hon. Joseph G. Kendall (an excellent man I afterwards found him,) was appointed successor to Mr. Bigelow, and administered the oaths and read the documents in his own natural tone of voice. The lawyers, with their green bags, were the subjects of my admiration ; they used to walk into court with such an air of consequence ; and were so busy, most of them in doing nothing. Most of the trials were conducted by Mr. Merrick and Mr. Allen ; and I could never understand the reason why they must get into a quarrel in almost all the cases they tried ; especially as they seemed to be good natured enough when the trial was over. I have since learned that many of the personal altercations in this world are only in a Pickwickian sense.

"They will have to build a new court house soon," said my father, as we passed out of Lincoln Square, and made our entrance into Main street. "Why, what for?" was the inquiry I naturally made. "Well," said he, "it has been so from the beginning. A public building does not serve well more than one or two generations before a new one is demanded to suit the wants and the taste of the people." He told me that the first court house was built the year after the county was incorporated; and I have since learned that the county was incorporated in 1731, by taking portions of the counties of Suffolk, Middlesex, and Hampshire. Worcester itself was in Middlesex. He said that the first court house was built of wood, and much resembled the country school houses (which are apt to stand where four roads meet;) and that the land was given by a Mr. William Jennison, who lived a little south of it. "Your grandfather," said he, "often told what a great day they had when the first court house was dedicated. People came into town from all parts of the county, and the exercises out of doors were full of fun : while within they consisted mainly of a speech from one of the judges." I have since discovered that the judge who made the speech, was Judge John Chandler, of Woodstock, now a town in Connecticut. That court house, my father said, much as it was praised at the time, lasted but about twenty years, when a second one, much larger, was erected. The second one, he well remembered, after being in service about fifty years, was moved from Court Hill to the head of Green street, where it was converted into a dwelling house, and is now the residence of George A. Trumbull, Esq.,* who, from the many anecdotes I have heard of him, must have been the residuary legatee of all the wits who flourished in the building during its half century of use as a court house. My father said that he took great interest in the building of the brick court house, and went often to see the progress made by the masons and carpenters ; and that he, with a multitude more, attended the dedication in the autumn of 1803, (I think he said it was,) when if I do not misremember, a eulogistic speech was delivered upon the grandeur and magnificence of the edifice, by the excellent Chief Justice, Robert

*This building is still standing in Trumbull Square.

Treat Paine, whose residence, I think, must have been at that time in Newburyport.

The brick court house, although now occupied by some of the lower courts, has been thrown into the shade by the elegant court house, with its six massive columns, all of hammered Quincy granite, standing in a commanding position a few rods south of the old house. But your readers know where and what it is without my telling them.

My father told me that in the early times of the county, Court Hill was more abrupt than it now is; that it seemed to him to be the head of a bank of gravel and sand that lies at the base of the clayey hill that runs along the whole length of the west side of Main street; that on its sloping sides grew native bushes; and on its summit stood the pillory, the whipping post and the stocks; and that when the poor rogues were punished, the boys, the men, and even women, were accustomed to gather around them, and make them the subject of rude witticism and coarse remark. "What is a pillory? What is a whipping post? What are the stocks?" were the questions I put to my father in quick succession. "I will tell you some time, but not now," said he ; and we went on our tour.

My father told me afterwards that he never saw but one pillory; and then a man and a woman were punished by standing in it one hour, to answer the sentence of the court. It consisted of a staging several feet above the ground, with a post rising in the centre. On the post were cross pieces with holes in them sufficiently large to admit the neck and wrists. The cross pieces were in two parts, so that the head and hands could be put into the holes; and, when in, they were brought together, encircling the neck and wrists; and there by the hour stood the culprits with their hands elevated as high as their heads, in danger of suffocating unless they stood straight up all the time; and there, all the while, they took the taunts and jibes of the spectators.

"I never saw but one man publicly whipped," said my father, "and he was a horse thief." He said that a post was set up in the ground, with a bar across it, higher up than a man's head. The thief was led out of jail by the officers, at a time of day when his punishment would be an admonition to as many spectators as possible; and when brought to the post he was stripped naked to his waist, and his hands tied up to the cross-bar. One of the officers then gave him as many lashes with the cat-o'nine-tails as the court had ordered, upon his naked back. The cat consisted of a whip handle about a foot and a half in length, with nine small knotted cords, of about the same length. My father said that the blood spurted out of the poor fellow's back, at the first blow, wherever the knots hit him. He shrieked out at every blow. He received fifteen lashes ; and when about half of them had been given, my father said it made him shudder to hear the sheriff exclaim to the officer : — " Cut harder, or I'll cut you !" He said that when the fifteen lashes had all been given, the blood ran freely down the culprit's back, which looked as red as raw beef ; and they then rubbed it over with soft soap, and led him back to prison.

There were other punishments administered by the courts in the olden times. My father said that he never saw a prisoner in the stocks ; nor did he ever see the cropping of ears ; but he remembered to have seen persons whose ears had suffered some curtailment by the application of the legal shears. Another punishment was that of branding. He said that he saw it done once. A thief was taken from jail to a place where all who wanted could witness the

operation.   He was laid upon his back in a rough
box ; his hands and feet secured ; and the letter T
pricked into his forehead with indelible ink.   There
it stood, not a " scarlet letter," but an ugly black one
in the face and eyes of the world ; and years of
penitence could not efface it, nor " sorrow's tear,"
coursing through a life of bitter remorse, wash it out.

                          Yours,

                                    CARL.

CHAPTER VII.

Mr. Editor: — What was the subject of my last chapter? Oh, I remember; it was about court houses, pillories, whipping posts, and stocks, and lawyers, and such paraphernalia of courts of justice. My father told me that he had often heard my grandfather represent the condition of things which prevailed here when the courts were first held in Worcester, a century and a quarter ago. Every term of the courts,— and it made no difference whether it was the supreme or an inferior court,— was a holiday. All the jockeys in the county came in; and Main street from one end to the other, was a common race-course, until it had become such an unendurable evil to the inhabitants, that an ordinance was adopted which imposed a fine of 20 shillings upon any one who should race a horse through Main street while any court was in session.

At that time the inferior court was composed of a chief justice, and all the magistrates in the county as side-judges; and my father said that he heard my grandfather tell how he once went into the court house when the court of sessions was sitting; and how he had with him a fine, large, black Newfoundland dog. Old Gen. Ruggles was on the bench as chief justice, with a row of inferiors extending out each side of him. The chief had no respect for a court thus constituted; and when my grandfather's dog mounted himself, uninvited, in a vacant chair among the judges, Judge Ruggles turned upon the dog, and in a blunt manner exclaimed to him: — "Get down out of that chair, upon the floor, and presume not to seat yourself there again, *before you have taken the oath!*" This anecdote reminds me of a similar judge of a like court, in our neighboring state of New Hampshire. They have side-judges there; and one of them said that he had never been consulted on the bench but once by the chief justice; and that was on one day at the close of a long term. The clerk was winding up the docket: there was a momentary suspension of business; and the chief justice turned to him and asked, in a complaisant manner: — " Is not this bench made of *hard* wood?"

My father said that he often heard his father remark that there was no lawyer in Worcester when the county was incorporated: that Josh. Eaton was the first one who ventured to put up his " shingle" here: that he came from some town near Boston, and although not a man of splendid abilities, he nevertheless did a good business and accumulated a handsome property; and, what was singular for one of that profession he was almost fanatical upon the subject of religion—practising law week days, and going up to what is now Spencer, to preach on Sundays.

My father said, and he seemed to know all about it, that there were several odd specimens of lawyers in Worcester in the early times, besides Josh. Eaton. Some of them kept stores, and sold cod-fish and molasses, and made writs, deeds, and pleas, just as their customers wanted. Yet there were some able men; Putnam, the Chandlers, Lincoln, and Judge Bangs. The latter my father said was a man of talent and taste: lived for a long time in a house, with his office attached to it, opposite where the stone court house now stands, and where the " Bangs Block " has been recently erected; and in the rear of which he had a large and beautiful garden in which he had a splendid

collection of fruits and flowers that were beautiful and
rare for those times.

Perhaps my love for historical studies was to some
extent developed by hearing my father often allude to
the "Shays Rebellion," which took place when he
himself was a boy. He remembered its scenes and
events with the certainty of an eye witness; and as it
was in his early life, they planted themselves deep in
his memory. I have not the time, nor is it necessary,
to enter into any explanation of the causes that produced that civil war in our midst. Suffice the remark,
that the country had just come out of the eight years'
war of the revolution. It was impoverished by taxation.
Property, if sold at all, was sold at an immense sacrifice.
My grandfather used to sell wood, which grew at no
great distance from his house, for 50 dollars the cord,
and corn at 15 dollars the bushel; and my father said
that he went out once with him, and helped him drive
home a cow, for which he paid 750 dollars, in the
currency of the times. Everything was on the "high
road to ruin." Debts could not be paid; and the
more they could not, the more the lawyers made
writs, so that in the two years preceding the "Shays
Rebellion," nearly 4000 suits were entered in the courts

4

of Worcester county, notwithstanding the population
was but about one-third as large then as it now is.
The people were aroused well nigh to desperation;
and they determined that the courts should not pass
the writs to judgment and execution. I confess to a
good deal of sympathy with the public feeling of that
time, although they were in error. Meetings were
held in many of the towns. Conventions were called.
But it was not till the September term of the court of
common pleas, for the year 1786, that open resistance
was made to the administration of justice. The
Monday before the Tuesday on which the court was
to commence its term, it was rumored that a company
of soldiers were coming into town from Hubbardston,
to prevent the court from being held: and my father
said that he and a multitude more of boys and men
went out on the Holden road (what is now Salisbury
street,) to meet them. When first seen they were
coming down Pratt's hill, and looked rather formidable with their guns and bristling bayonets. They
halted, he said, for a moment opposite the Quigley
road, as though in expectation of resistance to their
farther progress. It was but for a moment, when
they passed on to Court Hill, in front of the court

house, where they were addressed by their captain, Adam Wheeler, and where many who sympathized in the movement came forward and gave them their congratulations. The company was nearly a hundred strong. They surrounded the court house, and took possession. They made their headquarters, as I have before stated, at the " Hancock Arms," which stood on Lincoln street. Early the next morning a company, under Captain Smith, marched into town on the same road, and joined Wheeler's men at the court house. At the appointed hour, the judges with the old Chief Justice Ward at their head, sheriffs, lawyers, etc., moved through Main street in a body. My father said he was standing in the bushes that then grew on the bank in front of the court house, where he could see what was done, and hear what was said. A file of soldiers stood at the door with bayonets fixed, and the house was filled with armed men. He said his blood curdled when he saw the old general judge stopped at the door by the bayonets which were pressed against his bosom ; but that in no way daunted he ordered the soldiers to fall back, and the door to be opened. Neither party gave way ; and for a long time the judge stood resting against the bayonets, all the while talking in a loud tone about the laws and the gallows. After making a long speech, the judges retired from the court house to the "United States Arms," (now the Exchange Hotel,) where the court was regularly opened, and adjourned to the next day. The rebellion forces increased through the day and night, and were known by the little sprigs of evergreen stuck in their hats. The court found itself shut out from the court house, and adjourned its term to November.

In November the court met with the same sort of resistance, and adjourned without transacting any business. It is not my purpose to write a history of the " Shays Rebellion," because it may be found detailed at length in the records of the times, and by the diligence and fidelity of subsequent historians. But my father said that when the court met again in November, he expected that there would be a battle ; as the insurgent troops were on hand in great numbers, and the military companies of the town had turned out to uphold the courts. The judges then found that the rebellion troops had taken possession of the "United States Arms" for their headquarters, and they were compelled to open their court at the old "Sun Tavern" which stood on the ground now occupied by the splendid block of stores recently erected by William C. Clark.* The military of the town formed on the common, and marched down Main street. My father said he run by their side, and that when they had come to within a few rods of the "U. S. Arms" they found the way blocked up by the insurgent forces. Both forces looked resolute ; both seemed determined to fight for the mastery ; and every moment he expected to hear the bullets whistle. But fortunately the rebellion men gave way, and retreated to Court Hill, and the court troops passed on to the "Hancock Arms." No business was attempted by the court, which adjourned over to January. Yet the insurgents were not to be tired out by adjournments ; and it was in the first week in December, (1786) that Shays made his entrance into town at the head of about 800 men from the county of Hampshire and the western part of Worcester. Their appearance was imposing, my father said, as they drew up in front of the court house. But as there was no special occasion for their presence here, they marched back the next day as far as Rutland, in the

*Now known as the Walker Building, at the corner of Main and Mechanic sts.

midst of a severe snow storm, some of them perishing by the way from cold and hunger.

As the time approached for the holding of the court which had been adjourned to the last of January, Governor Bowdoin determined to adopt vigorous measures. An army of 4400 men, from the five counties of Suffolk, Essex, Middlesex, Hampshire and Worcester, was called into service for one month ; and the whole placed under the command of Gen. Benjamin Lincoln. The three regiments from Suffolk, Essex and Middlesex, marched out of Boston and encamped the first night in Marlborough ; and reached Worcester in the afternoon of the next day. The town presented a truly warlike appearance for a usually quiet country village. It was the dead of winter, and every house was full of armed men. General Lincoln, the next day, left General Warren, of Hampshire, in command at Worcester, with a regiment of troops to protect the court, while he moved on with the main body of his forces towards Springfield. Shays had retreated to Pelham, and again to Petersham. Advised of his position, Lincoln moved by a forced march from Hadley to Petersham, a distance of more than thirty miles, in a single night, in the midst of a snow storm. Shays and his men, surprised at their unexpected approach, fled in consternation in every direction. Some of the insurgents were tried; most of them acquitted; and others treated with lenity by the government.

Daniel Shays was no ordinary man. My father said that he never saw but few men who excelled him in the qualities of a popular leader. Mounted on a large white horse, he looked finely as he rode down Salisbury street at the head of his regiment of 800 men. His birthplace was "Saddle Hill" in the westerly part of Hopkinton, in Middlesex. But his family moved when he was young into western Massachusetts, and it was there that he enlisted in the revolutionary army, in which he did good service as a captain. On retiring from the war he settled in Pelham in Hampshire; and there he was visited by the leaders of the rebellion, and induced to take the command of their forces. Shays fled into Vermont; and from there he moved into York State where he died, in the town of Sparta, about thirty years ago.

I think better of Shays than the world has generally thought of him. I am no advocate for rebellion; but I must believe that under the circumstances, the courts, and especially the lawyers, should have shown more indulgence than it appears they did show to the people in the terrible embarrassments in which they had been placed by the eight years' war. Writs were followed by executions; and executions by forced sales, in which the property sold for scarcely more than enough to pay the costs. Shays's purpose, mistaken though he may have been, was nothing beyond a reform of what were deemed the abuses of government. But he was deceived by those in whom he had confided. The people did not rally under his pine tree banner as he was assured they would; and thus a movement which opened with the solemn significance of a tragedy, closed with all the mock heroism of a farce. This is a portion of the history of our Main street: written sixty-nine years ago — not with fire and blood upon the ground, but upon the memories of the people.

Yours,

CARL.

CHAPTER VIII.

Mr. Editor:—Twenty years ago there stood upon the precise ground now occupied by the stone court house, the dwelling house of one of the most remarkable men of Massachusetts. His name was known throughout the whole country. He died about a quarter of a century ago, and not many years after his decease, his house was removed to a lot in the rear, where it now stands; but the stately appearance it had in my boy days, has been marred by the removal. It was the house of Isaiah Thomas. My father said that he knew him well, and was intimate with him, and in early times they had extensive dealings with each other. Just south of his house stood his office, where he carried on the printing business more extensively than any other man in the country; employing, at times, not less than one hundred and fifty hands in the various departments of making paper, and printing, and binding, and selling books, newspapers, etc.   Printing was all done in those times by hand presses, and without the aid of the complicate and beautiful machinery which later inventions have introduced.

Although my father was younger than Dr. Thomas, and was but a boy at the time, he said he remembered well the day when the Declaration of Independence was received in town ; that it was soon noised abroad that such a document had come in the southern mail ; and that the citizens of the town, and others from the country who happened to be in town, gathered in large numbers at the Old South Church.* Dr. Thomas went into the porch, and taking a Philadelphia newspaper from his pocket, read the declaration in a clear and loud tone of voice ; putting special emphasis upon some portions of the document, and nodding his assent to those passages that were considered as particularly severe upon the conduct of

*The messenger bearing the Declaration of Independence to Boston, passed through Worcester on the 14th of July, and was intercepted and a copy obtained, which was read, as above stated, from the porch on the west side of the Old South Meeting House. The Declaration was first printed in New England in the Spy of July 17.

old King George. With a flushed countenance he concluded the reading, and then called upon the assembly to give three cheers for the Continental Congress. It was then proposed that the clergyman be requested to read the declaration in the pulpit the following Sunday; and that a patriotic meeting be held on the common the Monday succeeding. My father said that most of the persons present seemed to be wonderfully elated on the occasion ; but that he noticed a little knot of well dressed gentlemen who looked pale, haggard and dejected, while the document was being read ; and that when it was over they went across the road by themselves, and were engaged in earnest conversation for a long time. I do not remember what he said of them, farther than that they were tories who disapproved of the declaration, and thought that the country had been ruined by a rash and radical congress.

The next Sunday, my father said he was early at church. Every one was talking of the news. The minister read the declaration in the pulpit. Many of the congregation seemed to be much pleased with it ; others looked sad and disheartened ; while very many appeared to be in doubt whether to approve or not.

And that was the first reading of the Declaration of Independence in the churches.

The next day the people gathered together in great numbers upon the common.   The bell was rung ; cannons and muskets were fired ; and all the machinery of a modern 4th of July was put in motion ; and a master-spirit in the movement was Dr. Thomas.   The arms of George III. were brought from the court house, and burned upon the common ; and the people then formed a procession, and moved to the music of a drum and fife to the " King's Arms" tavern, which stood where the Worcester House* now stands, and requested the good landlady to take down her sign, which had the king's arms painted upon it, and use it to kindle her oven with.   She readily complied with their request, and they closed the ceremonies by drinking toasts appropriate to the occasion.

Dr. Thomas manifested at an early age his repugnance to British authority.   After serving his apprenticeship to a printer in Boston, he went to Halifax in Nova Scotia, into the office of the Halifax Gazette. But it was not long before he became involved in difficulty.   The Gazette was the government paper ;

*Now the Lincoln House.   These proceedings took place on the 22d of July.

its paper was sent out stamped from England; and Thomas took the liberty to cut off the stamps before putting it to press. He returned to Boston, and commenced the publication of the " Massachusetts Spy." But as the revolutionary spirit began to burn, he moved from Boston to Worcester, where he built up the large business I have already mentioned. In all the war measures he took an active part. He was the first postmaster in Worcester, and was largely identified in all public movements, in which he was liberal as well as public-spirited. He made several donations to the town. It must have been half a century ago that he opened, built and dedicated to the public use, the street that bears his name; for my father was accustomed to relate what a jovial time they had; the soldiers marching through the street and firing volleys; and the people bringing out their pailsful of punch, which was freely distributed.

I have already mentioned Dr. Thomas as the founder of the American Antiquarian Society, and the liberal donor of the land and building, and of the great mass of books, papers and pamphlets, which he had accumulated in the prosecution of his business. I have seen an extract from his will which evinces the kind interest which he manifested for the poor and unfortunate. After donating a piece of land on Thomas street — I think it was opposite the Thomas school house — on condition that the town should erect an almshouse thereon, he provided that $20 a year should be taken from the income of the investment to furnish a good Thanksgiving dinner to the pauper inmates, with half a pint of wine to each one, or such spirituous liquors as they might prefer. The town declined to accept the donation; and, so far as I know, the paupers have to this time been without the wine and spirits they would otherwise have received.

Dr. Thomas's remains were deposited in the granite tomb, near the Boston and Worcester railroad track, in the old burying ground on the north side of Mechanic street.* Some of his descendants are among us, filling high places in the public service, and in the esteem of the people.

As we passed by the Thomas house, my father pointed out the spot where the first school house in

*Dr. Thomas's remains, with the stone tomb in which they were inclosed, were removed to Rural Cemetery, June 24, 1878.

Worcester was erected. He said it was standing there when he was a boy. The ground about has been so changed since, that I am not able now to identify the spot; but it was near the middle of Main street, nearly opposite the Thomas house; and was passed by us shortly after we went out of Lincoln Square into Main street. Whatever may have been the changes in the locality of business and of population, it is manifest that the " North End" has its full share of historic memories and associations.

Yours,

CARL.

CHAPTER IX.

Mr. Editor :—"That is a very nice church," said I to my father, as we passed along from the Thomas house, and came to the meeting house of the Second Parish, the next building south.

"Yes," was his reply; "we thought so when it was built; and there is my old friend Dr. Bancroft, the minister, standing upon the steps." We stopped, and they talked a few minutes together. The doctor was talkative and pleasant, but serious in his air. I had seen him in the pulpit, but had never before heard him speak elsewhere. I remembered him as he prayed in church with his eyes wide open and fixed upon some point, and of his simple and effective earnestness in preaching; and in my limited vision he was always associated with my idea of the "great apostle to the Gentiles," St. Paul. It was the remark of my father, I remember, that "he is an intellectual man, of a great share of common sense, of simplicity and force of character, and who cares less for himself than he does for the people, to whom he is supremely devoted. It was about fifty years ago," he said, "that Dr. Bancroft came to Worcester to live." And he told me that the doctor was then about thirty years of age; of middle stature, dark complexion, slender, and straight. There was but one meeting house in town, which was then all one parish. You remember that in a former chapter I spoke of the destruction, by a mob of "gentlemen," of a house of worship which had been erected in the upper part of Lincoln street, by the Scotch Presbyterians, who settled here about the year 1718; among whom was the Irish James Rankin, the father of the beautiful Anna Rankin, who married the young collegian, Sam. Andrews, whose daughter, Anna Andrews, was the wife of Col. Timothy Bigelow, the patriot blacksmith of the revolution. "When they tore that meeting house down," said my father, "they meant to put a stop forever to all dissensions in the church, and retain the whole town in support of one meeting; and they succeeded for more than half a century. But they

5

could not chain the human mind up to one form of belief, however important it might be in itself; nor fetter the conscience with the shackles of opinions which some men held to be true, but which others did not believe in." The attention of the whole people was so much engrossed by the war that they had no leisure for church quarrels; and things went on harmoniously until the peace of 1783 gave the people an opportunity to turn their attention in a greater degree to spiritual matters; and then, as is too often the case, the beauties and graces of the Christian life were too often marred and disfigured by bickerings about minor points of doctrine or form.

My father said that when a boy he was required to go to meeting every Sunday, rain or shine; and as the minister of the Old South Church, Rev. Thaddeus Maccarty, was for him a dull preacher — perhaps because the infirmities of age were coming upon him — he was glad when they began to talk about having a new minister. Mr. Bancroft preached, and a part of the town were anxious to settle him as a colleague with Mr. Maccarty. But there was a strong party opposed to him. They thought he was unsound on some points of belief; and that, although a good man, his settlement would open the door for heresies to creep in. The contest grew warm, and ended only in the withdrawal of some of the church, and of many of the parish, who formed a separate society and invited Mr. Bancroft to become their minister.

Several of the prominent men of the town left the old church and joined the new parish; among whom, I remember to have heard my father say, were the elder Levi Lincoln, Judge Bangs, Col. Timothy Bigelow and Isaiah Thomas; and if I remember aright it was about the year 1785 that they met for the first time for separate worship, in the court house (now the Trumbull house), where they continued to hold their meetings for a period of six or seven years. They drew up and signed a church covenant. It was in February, 1786, that Dr. Bancroft was ordained; and at that time there were but two settled ministers in the county whom it was thought it would be of any use to invite to the ordination — Rev. Mr. Harrington, of Lancaster, and Rev. Mr. Adams, of Lunenburg. The other clergymen who took part in the ordination exercises, were from Boston and Salem.

While this young church was struggling into life, its members were obliged, not only to support it from their purses, but to pay the taxes that were assessed upon them by the town for the support of the gospel at the old church. This hardship induced the second parish to procure the passage of the Act of 1787, which permitted persons to quit one society and join another by filing a notice of their intention with the clerk. After worshiping in the court house for half a dozen years, the second parish gained strength sufficient to build a meeting house. It was built of wood, on the east side and near the north end of Summer street; and was occupied by the parish until the year 1829, when the brick building, spoken of at the commencement of this chapter, was completed. At the time I made my tour through Main street the old meeting house had lost its identity as a church. The porch has been cut off, and moved out at a mile or more on the Grafton road, and been converted into a negro-man's dwelling house. The church itself had been metamorphosed into a hotel — what in later times would be denominated a "rum tavern." Failing to make itself profitable at that, it underwent another change, was sold to the town, and converted

into a school house ; for which commendable purpose
it is now employed ; though when I reflect on the
adamantine endurance of school house associations,
I could wish, for the sake of the young minds that
go there for illumination, that it had a pleasanter
location.*

The brick church " served its day and generation,"
which expired in 1849. The organ had been taken
out of the house, and extensive repairs had been just
completed, when one fine summer evening, just before
9 o'clock, it was discovered that the church was on
fire. The fire mounted rapidly to the belfry, and
up the steeple, beyond the reach of the firemen ; and
in a short time the building was a pile of ruins ; in
which was a bell nearly new, of a finer tone than any
Worcester ever had before or since. To a person who
has an eye for the picturesque, it was worth the price
of the building to see the flames as they darted up
and curled and twisted, like so many fiery serpents
bent on mischief, around the timbers that formed the
steeple ; consuming their substance as they played,
until timbers and serpent flames fell into darkness
together.

*This building is standing on Summer street, and is still used as a school-house.

"Did they save the commandments?" inquired a merry wag of me the next morning, as I stood looking over the ruins. And he then told me that he alluded to the tablets which hung at the sides of the pulpit, on which were written in letters of gold the Ten Commandments; and how the prince of wits who painted them had inquired of one of the good deacons of the church, if in painting them he would not prefer to have them clear boards with all the *nots* left out.

It is now nearly seventy years since the second parish became a distinct religious community; and during all that time it has embraced a liberal share of the prominent men of the town. It has never had but two ministers, Dr. Bancroft and the present officiating clergyman.* The new house will justify me in applying to it the designation of a "nice church" which I applied to the old one twenty years ago. Church building, like too many church-goers, seems to have a sensibility to fashion and keeps up with its progress. What will meet the demands of future generations it will be for a future historian to record.

Yours.   CARL.

---

*Rev. Alonzo Hill, D. D., who died Feb. 1, 1871.

CHAPTER X.

Mr. Editor:—Nearly opposite the church of the second parish, stands the Exchange Hotel, which has undergone scarcely any perceptible change during the twenty years that have passed since I made my tour in Main street, except in its name. Its sign then was, I remember, the "Exchange Coffee House, Samuel B. Thomas," and him I have not forgotten, with his capacious white hat and green spectacles. There were no railroads then. Most people travelled in stage coaches. It was a pleasure to me then to watch the stages as they came into town from Springfield and Northampton and Boston. Leaving the two places in the West they would arrive in town in season for the passengers to dine at the Exchange Coffee House; frequently eight or ten coaches full, inside and out;

and after dinner away one after another to Boston. Those were undoubtedly great times for country taverns on great roads : but they are gone, never to come back.

As we passed by the Exchange Coffee House, it was the remark of my father that he remembered perfectly well just how President Washington looked the morning that he stopped there to take his breakfast. It was the first year of his presidency—the first under the constitution. It was on Friday, the 23d day of October, 1789. The town, my father said, was thrown into a great excitement the afternoon previous by the arrival of the news that Washington was at Brookfield, and would reach Worcester the next morning. Every good horse was put in requisition ; and at sunrise a cavalcade of some forty to fifty gentlemen—most of them young men—rode up to Leicester, to meet the president and escort him into town. My father said, with hundreds of others he was in waiting near the south church ; and that as the president came over the high ground near where the Oread Institute now is, a signal was given, and cannons were fired and the bell rung. The president rode in a chariot drawn by four beautiful bay horses, which were understood to be of his own raising on his Virginia estates ; and when he had reached the south end of Main street, he left his chariot and rode horseback through Main street to the United States Arms, (afterwards the Exchange Coffee House,) when he dismounted and partook of a breakfast. My father said that the people were much disappointed that the president could stop no longer ; but he apologized by saying that it was then Friday morning, and he was anxious to reach Boston before Sunday. After breakfast, amidst immense cheering by the people who had assembled in great numbers, Washington took his seat in his chariot, and started off on the old road to Boston (now Lincoln street), attended as far as Marlborough by a large cavalcade of gentlemen from Worcester.

Washington was then 57 years and 8 months old. He wore a brown dress, my father told me ; and was an unostentatious, plain, sedate citizen, notwithstanding people generally addressed him and spoke of him as *His Highness the President.* And I may as well relate, in passing, how this title happened to be applied to Washington. When on his way from Virginia to New York, previous to his inauguration, he stopped to dine at the house of Dr. Shippen in Philadelphia.

Several gentlemen were at the table,—among whom was Mr. Madison and Judge McKean, Mrs. Shippen inquired what was to be the TITLE of the president. Some one suggested that of *His Serene Highness;* but as that was appropriated abroad, it was discarded. A discussion arose upon the propriety of any title. Mr. Madison thought that nothing could be so appropriate, and so much in keeping with the character of our republican institutions, as the plain designation, *The President.* Judge McKean went in strong for a title, and suggested that of *His Highness.* Washington himself was in favor of some title, and intimated the pertinency of that of the Stadtholder of Holland, *His Mighty Highness.* But Judge McKean's suggestion met with the most favor; and if the title was to have been perpetuated, it is fortunate that nothing more resplendent was adopted, as it would be ludicrously inapplicable to some little men who are sometimes found in big places.

I am tempted here to introduce a letter written by Washington, at Hartford, when on his way home from his eastern tour. He did not come back through Worcester; but went by the way of Uxbridge. It was written to a Mr. Taft, thus:

" *Sir* :—Being informed that you have given my name to one of your sons, and called another after Mrs. Washington's family, and being moreover much pleased with the modest and innocent look of your two daughters *Patty* and *Polly*, I do for these reasons send each of these girls a piece of chintz ; and to Patty, who bears the name of Mrs. Washington, and who waited upon us more than Polly did, I send five guineas, with which she may buy herself any little ornaments she may want, or she may dispose of them in any other manner more agreeable to herself. As I do not give these things to have it talked of, or even to its being known, the less there is said about the matter the better you will please me ; but that I may be sure the chintz and money have got safe to hand, let Patty, who I dare say is equal to it, write me a line informing me thereof, directed to ' The President of the United States, New York.' I wish you and your family well, and am your humble servant."

As this was long before my day—and I do not remember even to have heard my father speak of it—I never heard what was said of the chintz dresses given to Patty and Polly Taft by President Washington, nor what disposition Patty made of her five guineas, which she received in consideration of her having been named after *Miss Martha Dandridge*. It would please me much, Mr. Editor, and I doubt not the information would be acceptable to your readers, if some one who has the facts would inform us what became of Patty and Polly ; for it is manifest, from his letter, that Washington, as the saying is, "took quite a shine" to Patty.   I hope she received the chintz and the money all safe ; and that she wrote an acknowledgement of their reception, as she was desired to do.

I know not what may have been the various fortunes of the 'United States Arms'—whether it was altered, enlarged, or rebuilt,—after Washington left it on that Friday morning, the 23d of October, 1789; for my personal knowledge of it covers but about one-third of its intervening history.   But I remember that it was reputed to be an excellent hotel, furnishing " refreshments for man and beast;" among which were those " refreshments" which too many *men* are fond of, but which *beasts* will not take at all.   I remember, also, that twenty years ago, as I was passing by one morning I discovered that there had been a sudden conversion on the premises ; that the old sign had been pulled down, and a new one elevated in its place ; and that without an act of the legislature or a decree of the judge of probate, the hotel had dropped its savory name of " Exchange Coffee House" for the significant one of " Temperance Exchange."

And on a post, near by, I read a proclamation of the fact of the conversion, by the proprietor, in which he invited all the friends of the " noble cause of temperance" to come forward and sustain his house in the new life on which it had just entered. I am not able to say when this incident occurred ; but it is my impression that it was shortly after the passage of that famous law which provided that men should take ardent spirits in no less quantities than fifteen gallons at a time. Judging from outward indications, the old " United States Arms," where the judges opened their court when repelled from the court house by the Shays men, and where as president of the United States, Washington took breakfast five years after he congratulated himself that he had gone forever into the quiet retreat of private life; judging from outward indications, I say, I think it can have prospered but indifferently under some of its modern metamorphoses.

Yours,

CARL.

CHAPTER XI

Mr. Editor :—It was the remark of my father that the old " United States Arms" was a favorite resort of travellers; though many found accommodations at the other public houses. Previous to the year 1783, people travelled in their own private carriages ; those who travelled at all ; and consequently good inns, at short intervals on the great roads were more numerous and more necessary than they now are. In twelve hours the traveller may now journey from New York to Philadelphia. My grandfather went once to Philadelphia, as I have heard my father say, in company with the mail carrier, and returned with him. It must have been a century ago, at least. They were three weeks on the road, when going, and the same length of time when returning; so that it then took six weeks to make the out and in journey, which in these days of steam, can be made in but little more than twenty-four hours. It was about twenty years afterward that a regular stage was established between Boston and New York, by a Boston gentleman of the name of Brown. His running time from city to city was fixed at thirteen days, and the stages left each city once in two weeks. But it met with so little encouragement that it was soon discontinued; and the mails were carried, as before, in saddle bags on horseback. Two of the post-riders, my father said, he well remembered. I think their names were Hyde and Adams; their route was between Boston and Hartford; and when coming into town it was their custom to blow their post-horns, to notify the people of their coming. They stopped at the "United States Arms," and carried their saddle bags to Isaiah Thomas's office, for him to change the mails.

It was on the return of peace in 1783, that the project of a line of stages between Boston and New York was revived by Levi Pease and Reuben Sikes of Connecticut. Their starting point in Boston was the old "Lamb" tavern which stood in close proximity with the "Lion," if I remember rightly what was told me, on the spot, I believe, now occupied by the "Adams House." They commenced with light

wagons; running the first day from Boston to North-
borough; the second day to Brookfield; and occupying two days more to Hartford. From what my
father told me of Mr. Pease and Mr. Sikes, I
should infer that they were men of energy and enterprise; and if I am not in error, they in time had
regular lines of coaches running all the way from
Boston to Savannah in Georgia. Mr. Sikes was the
landlord of the Exchange Coffee House for many
years; and in that capacity, as well as an owner and
manager of numerous lines of stages that run between
Worcester and Boston, Hartford, etc., his history is
part of the history of our Main street.

Passing by the Exchange Coffee House, we came
to the building which has been long known as the old
Green Store*; and my father said that when he was
a boy he had a pair of corduroy pants and a fustian
jacket, which was manufactured in that building.
My recollection is that it was in the latter part of the
revolution when it was thought worth the while to
attempt the experiment of manufacturing cloths like
some of the coarse articles that had formerly been im-
ported from England. Some of the prominent men

*Where Parker's Block now stands.

of the time associated together, and erected a factory, and put into it some rude machinery for carding and spinning. The factory stood upon Mill Brook, on or near the site where the School street mills now stand. They prospered indifferently well for several years, until the restoration of friendly relations between the United States and England enabled the country to supply itself with manufactured goods cheaper than it could manufacture them. The manufacture of Worcester corduroys and fustians declined, and was finally abandoned. The factory was shoved off its foundations, moved up to Main street, and, if I remember rightly, was converted into a store, and long occupied for the purposes of trade. I have never known much of the building or its occupants; but I fear that some have " spun yarns" there, and woven " corduroys" while on their way home, whose fate might have been better than it has been if the old " Green Store" had always remained a corduroy and fustian factory; for although I have not been in the building for many years, and should be unable to frame an indictment against it, I have often seen signs about it, indicative of the admonition that *the last days of that factory are worse than the first.*

6

Upon the principle of the association of ideas, I am reminded that the Maine Liquor Law is no novelty in Massachusetts, as many suppose that it is. It has fallen under my observation that the General Court, more than one hundred years ago, passed an act imposing a severe tax upon the consumption of spirituous liquors and wines, and compelling every householder, under a heavy penalty, to make oath, to the excise man, of the amount of each article consumed in his house. That was a stringent law, I confess; but I opine that the court cared more for the revenue it expected to derive, through the agency of the law, than for the morals of the community. Shirley was governor at that time; and he refused to sign the bill. It was printed for general information; and the town of Worcester, at a meeting held on the 2d day of September, 1754, voted that the bill ought not to become a law; and they instructed their representative, John Chandler, to oppose its enactment.

Yours,

CARL.

CHAPTER XII

Mr. Editor:—Whoever knew our Main street twenty years ago, will remember that nearly opposite the Exchange Coffee House, and next south of the First Unitarian Church, there stood a large square house, a little angling with the street, with a large yard in front, filled with flowers, and a spacious fruit orchard in the rear. There was also upon the front of the lot a long two-story wooden building which had once been a store, and was then occupied for mechanical purposes. If I remember aright, my father told me that the *National Ægis* was at one time printed in that building. But the march of improvement has been there, and I can see nothing there now which I saw then, except a few scattered fruit trees, which were probably saved for what they are instead of what they have been. I remember the owner and occupant; an aged and deaf man, Dr. Oliver Fiske. My father knew him well, and spoke to him at his

gate as he passed by.   He had in his hand a basket of
fruit which he had been picking; and he gave me
some delicious pears and apples as specimens of the
fine varieties which it had been his pleasure to cultivate more extensively than at any time they had
been cultivated by any other individual in this region.
Modern improvement is a great leveller.   It spares
neither taste nor past memories, in its all-grasping
struggle for the profits of speculation and trade.   State
street now runs where stood but a few years ago Dr.
Fiske's hearthstone.   Harvard street crosses through
his orchard; and houses now occupy his fruit grounds,
which, I dare say, never entered into the good doctor's most fanciful dreams.   "One generation builds,
and another teareth down."

It was the remark of my father, I remember, that
Dr. Fiske had long been one of the most prominent
men of Worcester; and that when he was only eighteen years old he left his father's parsonage in Brookfield, and enlisted into the Army of the Revolution,
and marched to West Point; not as young gentlemen
go to West Point in these times of peace, to play the
soldier and get an education at the public expense,
but to endure the rigors, the hardships, and the perils

of war. After the war was over, young Fiske — for
he could not have been more than one and twenty at
that time — entered Harvard College, where I find by
reference to the college catalogue, (which happens to
be lying near me as I write this on my hat), that he
graduated in 1787. My father told me also, that while
the doctor was in college, his "war spirit" would
sometimes break over the bounds of restraint; that he
was captain of a military organization among the college boys; and that when the Shays party undertook
to stop the courts at Concord, the college company,
with Fiske for captain,* volunteered their services to
march up there from Cambridge, in aid of the government; and that there was a great tumult among the
boys when the college officers interfered and put a
veto on their quixotism. When the winter vacation
came, young Fiske took charge of a district school a
few miles from the college; and while enacting the
part of a village pedagogue, news came to him of the
mustering of the Shays men in Worcester. Turning
over his school to one of his college fellows, Fiske
came post-haste to Worcester, to take a part in the

___

*We think the writer is mistaken; and that Fiske was lieutenant and not cap-
tain of the college company.—ED.

conflict which seemed impending between the state government and its opponents. On arriving in Worcester, he found that the Shays men had retreated to the Connecticut river; and that leaving Gen. Warner here with one regiment of soldiers, for the protection of the court, Gen. Lincoln, with the main body of the army, had set off on a march to join Gen. Shepherd at Springfield, for the protection, not only of the courts there, but of the military stores, which it was supposed the Shays men would attempt to take. Young Fiske pushed on after them; and overtaking them on Leicester hill, he entered the ranks, and marched by his father's house in pursuit of the enemy. But fortunately he encountered no enemy to expend his surplus patriotism upon. Having completed his collegiate and medical education he located himself in Worcester, where he had a very considerable practice as a physician. He was, my father remarked, a man of a great deal of mental activity; took a deep interest in all associations and movements for public improvement; and withal was considerable of a politician; at one time holding a commission as a special justice of the court of common pleas; at another, and for several years in succession, being one of the governor's council ; and at a later period of his life, filling the office of register of deeds.   His deafness must have been a great misfortune to him, as its tendency must have been to abridge that activity of professional, social and civil life, for which he must have had many prominent qualifications.   Although he died but a few years ago, I apprehend that so great have been the changes in our population, there must be many among us at this day, to whom this brief sketch will seem to be more the product of fancy than of historical fact.

As we passed away from Dr. Fiske's we came to a spot on the Court Hill road that was then, as it now is, canopied with the branches of magnificient elms ; so thick that the noonday sun never falls upon the ground while the foliage is on the trees.   In such a town home for woodland nymphs I was led to make the inquiry of my father, "Who was it that set out the beautiful trees that line Main Street?"   His reply was that he had always understood that the principal mover in the matter was Dr. Elijah Dix.   If my memory of his remarks be true, Dr. Dix occupied the house* in front of which those four magnificient elms

*The site of this house is now occupied by the residence of F. H. Dewey.

stood, and that he it was who placed them there in the early part of his residence in Worcester. I regret deeply that any of these "ancient landmarks" should be obliged to give place to the passion for money-making, which seems to rule society with a terrific earnestness. But such is the fact: and I apprehend that the time is not far distant when there will not be a tree standing in Main street, from one end to the other. Pavements are laid without any apparent consideration for the life of the trees; and in some instances the propensity of the abutters, on the street, to appropriate, not only every part of their own land, but much of what belongs to the public, has crowded the trees beyond the sidewalks, and precluded the possibility of their occupying what has been perverted to coal-holes and other store conveniences. It is, in my view, a desecration of our Main street which ought never to have been permitted, and whose further progress the people ought to stay with a strong hand.

Dr. Dix, my father remarked, was a man of a scientific taste. He opened a medicine store near his house, as was not uncommon with the physicians of the last century: and there, although chemistry was then in its infancy compared to what it now is as a science, the doctor acquired a taste for compounding medicines, and chemical experiments, which induced him to visit Europe, for the attainment of knowledge, and for procuring the facilities for the prosecution of his scientific pursuits. After his return from Europe he moved from Worcester to Boston, where he engaged extensively in the sale of drugs and medicines, applying the knowledge he had acquired abroad to a chemical preparation of many of the articles he sold. As a prominent citizen of the town, which he put forth his taste and energy to adorn, during the latter part of the last century, Dr. Dix should have a grateful remembrance by our citizens ; for I am thinking that a people do honor to themselves when they do honor to their benefactors.

Yours,

CARL.

CHAPTER XIII.

Mr. Editor:—" And this is Granite Row," said my father, as we came to the block which at this time has almost ceased to bear the name. It had been erected a few years before by the late Hon. Daniel Waldo, on the spot, as I was informed, which had been long occupied by a less pretending building, and where by a long course of probity in dealing he made substantial additions to a fortune, considerable for his time, which had descended to him from his father. " Granite Row," which was designed to eclipse a block upon the opposite side of the street, and which in some degree measures what even a third of a century ago was regarded as bordering on the expensive, was then the centre of trade of Worcester. There were, it is true, twenty years ago, stores scattered in other parts of the town, but in " Granite Row," and in the stores opposite to it, nearly the whole dry-goods trade of the town was carried on. I see now but one sign remaining, of all those that then indicated the trade of that portion of the town ; and that belongs to the worthy gentleman* who kept then, as he keeps now, a hardware store in the south end of "Granite Row." The men of that day are gone, I scarcely know where. Some of them, through a constant repetition of their names in the columns of the weekly newspapers, made themselves known over the whole country, and profited by the trade which they attracted.

As we passed "Granite Row," I remember that my father pointed to the entrance into the chamber where two of the newspapers of the town were then printed. One of them was the *Massachusetts Yeoman ;* whose name, I suppose, indicated something of its character ; and the other, the *Worcester County Republican*, the organ of the "fierce democracy" which commenced cutting and thrusting its way into notoriety about the time that Gen. Jackson applied his iron nerves to the administration of the government. My father spoke of the editor of the *Yeoman* as a gentleman for whose memory he cherished the

*Henry W. Miller. Armsby Building covers a part of the site of Granite Row.

most kindly interest. It was Austin Denny; a native of Worcester, who died not long before, at the age of thirty-five. He had had a college education, and had been admitted to the bar. After officiating as editor of the *Spy* for three or four years, he established the *Yeoman*, which he published some seven years, until death relieved him from physical sufferings with which he had long been afflicted. It was the remark of my father, that "Austin, (as he always familiarly spoke of him), was not a brilliant or flashy writer; but was distinguished for candor, clearness and good common sense." The *Yeoman* survived its editor two or three years when it was merged into the *Ægis*. Of the *Republican*, I never had an intimate knowledge, and scarcely know its fate. Perhaps, Mr. Editor, you can enlighten those who have interest enough in the matter to raise the question.

Opposite "Granite Row," at the time I made my tour, a short, thick-set Frenchman kept a candy shop, which we boys were wont to patronize, and whose stories delighted me so much that I fear my puny exchequer suffered more from his humor than under other circumstances it would have done. His name I remember from a frequent perusal of the sign over his door, was Alexander Votier; and in his younger days he had served as a soldier in the armies of " Le Grand Napoleon;" of whom he had many stories to tell — some of which might have been true, and some of which might have been a little deficient in the first element of history. The old soldier had brought with him from the wars a penchant for " liquid fire," which when freely indulged in, " steals away the brain." Sitting behind his counter one warm summer evening, dosing in partial obliviousness, in popped a wag of a clerk from a neighboring store, disguised as a stranger, with the question : " Have you any chestnuts?"

" I vill see for de chestnut !" and after fumbling in all quarters he came to the conclusion that " de chestnut be all sold and gone."

" Sorry for it !" said the wag, " for I am in great want of a few." Then walking out, he went and changed his dress, and returning found Votier with head down again upon the counter, and again half oblivious of what was passing around him. Changing his voice, the clerk again made the inquiry: " Have you any chestnuts?"

" I am very sorry, but de chestnut be all gone. I vill have some more ver' soon."

Two or three times more the same application was repeated, under different disguises in the course of the evening; and the same half-stupified answer given; with the addition of, " Sorry dat I have got no chestnut, for everybody be wanting de chestnut dis evening."

" Have you any chestnuts this evening? Mr. Votier?" was the question which the merry clerk put as he entered the shop the last time. Returning consciousness let the light into the shopman's mind that his numerous customers for chestnuts were all one and the same individual; and, peeping up over his counter, the quondam soldier of Napoleon soon sent the young rogue tittering from the shop, with the benediction :

" You keep coming in here asking for de chestnut when you know dere is no chestnut. Dis is not de time of de year for de chestnut, and you knows it vell enough; and yet you come in here two, tree, six time, asking for de chestnut, chestnut. You go to ——, and get you chestnut ! You better man as you tink you are, by gar ! and if you dont behave yourself you'll soon get you chestnut *all ready roasted*, by gar !"

It was remarked by my father, that when the two-story brick block, opposite " Granite Row," which was called " Goddard's Row," was completed, the occupants had a grand illumination the first night they opened their stores. Every window was brilliantly lighted, and the crowd of people, that was present, was so large that it seemed to him that the whole town was there. Look upon that building, and then look upon the splendid blocks that were erected in 1854, and you have the materials for a comparison of the taste which then prevailed, and that which prevails now. I have a theory of my own upon the subject ; but this is not the occasion for me to moralize.

Next south of " Granite Row" stood twenty years ago, as now, what, when it was new, was known as " Waldo Church."* " They have got pretty much over their fight ;" said my father, as we passed by it ; and he then told me what he meant by the remark.

It seems hardly credible, at this day, that there could have been so much feeling excited as it seems there was between that church and the Old South Church, from which it was an offset, The circum-

---

*Central Church, now remodelled for business uses.

stances, as my father related them to me, have not
been treasured up by me as they would have been if it
had been a contest in which I take more interest than
I do in "the wars of Christians ;" but I presume that
its history has been written, and may be found in
the records of those times. It was about the year
1818 or 1819, that the south parish had settled a
new minister, the Rev. Charles A. Goodrich. The
church became divided in consequence. Several of
the members absented themselves from the commun-
ion ; and consequently were the objects of complaint ;
and, consequently again, they had their friends and
sympathizers ; and the more the fire was stirred, the
more it burned. It resulted in the organization of
the "Calvinist Church ;" which held its meetings in
the court house until 1823. In the mean time the
Hon. Daniel Waldo had erected a meeting-house at
his own expense, which cost if I am not mistaken,
about $15,000. He subsequently gave it to the so-
ciety, with the addition of $5000 in money, as a fund
for the payment, in part, of the parish expenses. The
house was dedicated, and Rev. Loammi Ives Hoadly
was ordained, at one and the same time ; and my
father remarked that there had been so much excite-

ment about the division that a great concourse of
people was present on the occasion. He said that
they had tried several candidates, before they obtained
one that suited them; and I remember that he spoke
in high terms of one of them, Rev. Thomas J. Murdoch, preferring him to Mr. Hoadly. He said that
Mr. Murdoch was a solid, substantial man; above
the ordinary size, and of dark complexion; but had
not quite so much of the "*suaviter in modo*," and
not quite so much fire and zeal as some of the ladies
of the parish desired to see in their preacher. Mr.
Hoadly's salary was fixed at $800 the year; and that
was considered quite liberal for the times.

For several years there was a feeling of bitterness
between the two churches; but as the town grew in
size, the feeling of acrimony grew less, and finally
died out. One of my earliest recollections of that
church, is, that after the society came into possession
of it, they greatly enlarged it by cutting it into four
quarters, moving the quarters apart, and filling in
between them, lengthwise and crosswise; and pro-
viding for what has become one of the largest and
most respectable religious societies of the city. It
does not comport with my purpose, in writing these

7

papers, to *praise the living*.   If it did, I should have a few words of praise for the fine scholar, the excellent citizen, and the consistent and liberal Christian, who now fills, with so much acceptance to his people, the pastorate of what was once known as "Waldo Church,"*

Yours,

CARL.

---

*Rev. Dr. Sweetser.

CHAPTER XIV.

Mr. Editor:—As I was walking in Main street the other day, I came up behind two of our aged and most respectable citizens; and heard one of them ask the other: "Who do you suppose that Carl of the Palladium is?" Of course I "pricked up my ears," and walked slowly behind them. The answer was: "I can not conjecture. I have thought of many persons, but am not able to fix on any one in particular as the writer." They both seemed anxious to know the humble individual who at that moment was so near to them that he could have touched them with his cane if he had had a cane. "His articles are very interesting," said one of them, "as they bring up to view scenes and persons that we were once familiar with." "Yes," said the other, "they do throw us back to times when Worcester was a very different

place from what it now is." And as the continuation
of his remark was rather more complimentary to myself than I care to listen to, I passed on, and walked
away from them, lest the interest I took in their
conversation might unfortunately betray me into an
exposure of my secret.

You will remember, Mr. Editor, that I do not
give the precise time of my tour in Main street. It
was about twenty years ago; and that is as explicit
as I choose to be upon the matter. At that time the
" *Spy Printing Office*" was the sign upon the building next south of the "Waldo Church." Messrs.
Earle & Colton, if my memory serves me, were then
the publishers. The *Spy* was then a valiant cham-
pion of whigism and the whig party, in the state and
in the nation; and for that reason, as well as for its
age, and the tact and ability with which it was conducted, it had an extensive circulation among the
people. My father said that he had been a constant
reader of the *Spy* for a long series of years; and he
gave me a running history of the paper. I cannot
presume to repeat all its details; and I have not access
to a file of the paper to correct my recollections.
I remember that he said that his old friend Isaiah

Thomas started the *Spy* in Boston, four or five years before the breaking out of the War of the Revolution ; and that immediately after the battle of Lexington, Mr. Thomas found himself unable to speak in Boston, (which was then in the hands of the British,) with the freedom with which he desired to speak of the action of the government ; and therefore, at the solicitation of Col. Timothy Bigelow, — the patriot blacksmith, whose love affair I chronicled in a former chapter — and other patriotic men, he moved the *Spy* from Boston to Worcester.* It was the acknowledged organ of the whigs of the Revolution ; and the leading men of that party made it a medium of communicating their sentiments to the people upon the crisis that was then impending. I may be in error, but my recollection is that my father said that when the *Spy* was first issued in Worcester, it was from a small building on Lincoln street, near to the " Hancock Arms" hotel ; and that it was there that Mr. Thomas leased it for a year to Messrs. Stearns & Bigelow, who published the paper from 1776 to 1777, while Mr. Thomas was closing up his business in Boston, Salem, etc., preparatory to a permanent residence in Worcester.

*It was moved to Worcester just *before* the battle of Lexington.

Mr. Stearns was a young lawyer who had just before opened an office in Worcester. It is said that he was a ready writer; and famed for his wit. Mr. Bigelow was also a lawyer; and, if I am not misinformed, he held the office of county attorney after the close of the Revolutionary War. After conducting the paper for a year they gave it up to a Mr. Haswell; and in 1778 he returned it to Mr. Thomas, who continued the publication, in connection with his other business, for a period of some twenty-five years. It is not my purpose to write a history of the *Spy*; for that can be done, when necessary, by my respected friend, the senior publisher,* who has been its editor for nearly one third of a century. May his shadow never be thinner! I remember well how he looked that day as my father and I passed by on our way to the cattle-show. He was standing in his office door, with a segar in his mouth, examining some apples which a countryman was showing him in a basket; and by his feet stood a box which appeared to be filled with beautiful sea-shells.

"This is the Baldwin place," remarked my father, as we came to the house next south of the *Spy* office,

*John Milton Earle.

and which is now in the possession of one* of the
venerable race of men that walked these streets, and
guided the destinies of our city when it was an unpretending hamlet.   Nathan Baldwin, my father told
me, was for a long time Register of Deeds for the
county of Worcester.   Old John Adams speaks of
him, in one of his letters, as one of the three "notable
disputants" in a religious controversy which raged in
the town when he came to Worcester to live in 1755.
I have seen his name in the records of the times as
one of the selectmen of the town in 1770, and its town
clerk from 1775 to 1778.   He was the associate of
Col. Bigelow and the other patriots of the day ; and
being a ready and forcible writer, as well as "notable
disputant," the task was assigned to him of drawing
up most of the documents which the town had occasion to use, before and during the Revolution, in
the form of instructions to the representatives in the
General Court, and protests against the arbitrary as-
sumptions and action of the crown.   It was while the
war was in its progress that the town passed a series
of resolves against speculations in produce and other

---

*William Eaton, whose daughter, Miss Sally Chadwick Eaton, died there in
June, 1887, aged 86.   This house at the corner of Main and George streets, is
now (1889) the oldest building in Worcester.

goods. I presume they were from Baldwin's pen; and they speak of them as "an augmented number of *locusts* and *canker-worms*, in human form, who have increased and proceeded along the road of plunder, until they have become obviously formidable, and their contagious influence dangerously prevalent — pestilential mushrooms of trade, which have come up in the night of public calamity, and ought to perish in the same night."

Baldwin was also one of the founders and leading spirits of the Political Society, a secret association of the prominent men of Worcester, which existed in the time of the Revolution, and rendered essential aid to the patriot cause by combining public sentiment, and giving direction and force to public opinion while the war was in progress. He died shortly after the peace of 1783; I have not the materials for an extended memoir of the man. He was evidently a man of talent, of intellectual force and moral courage. From the Adams letter I infer that by the prevailing religious denomination of the day, Baldwin was considered skeptical in his religious belief. Perhaps some of our citizens of to-day would feel a more lively interest in the man if they knew that as long ago as 1767, in penning instructions to the representative of that year, he used this remarkable expression : — " That you use your influence to obtain a law to put an end to that unchristian and impolitic practice of making slaves of the human species in this province."   And such was the language of a citizen of Worcester, nearly a century ago ; by whose last resting place two generations of men have passed, and a third is now in its progress.

Yours,

CARL.

CHAPTER XV.

Mr. Editor :— At the time I made my tour, there stood, as it stands now, on the east side of Main street, nearly opposite the " Waldo Church," an inn, hotel, tavern or public house, bearing the simple, and in those times, rather cold name of " Temperance House."* It was kept by Eleazer Porter, afterwards of the American House. " It used to be called the Blackstone Hotel," said my father, " in compliment to the Blackstone Canal :" which had been opened a few years before, from Worcester to Providence. It was not long afterwards that Main street was thrown into a prodigious excitement by the taking down of all the tavern signs in town, and the fastening up of the doors of all the public houses except the Tempperance House. On account of some refusal or delay to grant the customary license, the publicans, good

---

*This was at the corner of Thomas street.

souls, suddenly resolved that there should be "no more cakes and ale," nor rest for the weary traveller. Some travellers, in horror of a thing to which they were so unaccustomed as temperance, pertinaciously refused to eat, drink, or sleep in a temperance hotel, and sought and found refuge in private dwellings. While the public houses were thus in a state of "suspended animation," there was a fever of the public mind.   Men took sides, and "from words they almost came to blows."   I remember that one day as I was walking with my father, we came to a little knot of citizens who were standing not far from the Temperance House, in hot disputation about the new order of things.   My father was appealed to for his opinion; and while he was giving it, up came the good-humored, quick-witted librarian of the Antiquarian Hall (whom I spoke of particularly in a former chapter), and after listening for a moment, till there was a slight cessation of the "war of words," he peered at them over one corner of his spectacles, with the declaration :—" 'Ah, ye wicked and adulterous generation that seeketh after a sign!   But no sign shall be given unto you'— except that of Eleazer of the Temperance House!"   His good nature, thus oppor-

tunely exhibited, took all the starch of anger out of
the hot disputants ; and they quietly dispersed.   Since
that day the old Blackstone Hotel has been called the
Eagle Hotel and the Franklin House, and I know not
what else ; but never has it looked so trim, tidy and
inviting to me, as when it put out the unassuming
sign of the " Temperance House."

A few rods farther south we came to the residence
of the late Rev. Dr. Bancroft.*   I alluded to him in
my chapter on the church of the second parish, of
which he was so long the respected pastor.   I spoke
of him, venerable in appearance, as he seemed to me
the morning we passed him standing upon the steps
of his church ; and as I remembered him performing
the services of the sanctuary.   I remember of him
nothing but his old age, for his youth and manhood
were before my day.   Such brief memorials of him
as have come under my notice, ought to be combined
and elaborated, by some friendly hand, into an extended biography.   It is now nearly seventy years
since he was ordained in Worcester ; and had he lived
to the 10th of November next, his " life's span" would
have measured 100 years.   He was a collegian at

---

*Between Thomas and Central streets.

Cambridge when the War of the Revolution broke out; studied theology in his native town of Reading, with the Rev. Mr. Haven, its minister; and first came to Worcester in the autumn of 1783, to supply a temporary vacancy in the Old South Church, occasioned by the sickness of the Rev. Mr. Maccarty. On his death in the summer following, Mr. Bancroft was invited to return to Worcester and supply the pulpit again. But it was then discovered that there were differences of religious opinion in the church that disturbed the harmony of its action. Mr. Bancroft was unable to respond to the application until autumn. He then preached again for a few Sundays. As an evidence of the strength of the aversion that was felt in those times to a division of a church, it may be stated that a "compromise" was thought of, and deliberately proposed. It was to compromise all difficulties by settling two ministers — one for each party — the salaries of both to be paid from the parish treasury. Whether they were to "ride and tie" in preaching, or preach dialogues, I do not learn. But the proposition was not sustained.

The phrase, "ride and tie," which in these days of steam has well nigh fallen into disuse, had its ori-

gin in this way. Two travellers would go a journey
horseback, with only one horse for both. One would
ride two or three miles, and then dismount, hitch the
horse by the wayside, and walk on. His fellow-
traveller — for it would be an absurdity to call him a
companion — would mount the horse when he came
up to him; and this alternation gave origin to the
phrase, "ride and tie." It has given place to a new
set of phrases that may be designated not inaptly as
the literature of railroads.

The controversy ended, as all such controversies
usually do end, in a separation. A new church was
formed, and Mr. Bancroft was duly established as its
pastor. The covenant adopted at the time is a curiosity in its way, and inculcates the liberal and catholic
spirit with which the young pastor entered upon his
duties. I have met with nothing in its day that will
compare with it, and therefore, Mr. Editor, I beg to
trespass so far upon your indulgence, as to ask you to
copy it. It is thus : —

"In the first place, we humbly renew the dedication of ourselves and offspring to the great God,
who is over all, blessed for ever.

And we do hereby profess our firm belief of the
Holy Scriptures of the Old and New Testaments.

And taking them as our sole and sufficient rule of faith and practice, we do covenant to and with each other, that we will walk together as a Christian Society in the faith and order of the Gospel. And we do hereby engage, as far as in our power, for all under our care, that we will live as true disciples of Jesus Christ, in all good carriage and behaviour, both towards God and man. Professing ourselves to be in charity with all men who love Jesus Christ in sincerity and truth. All this we engage faithfully to perform, by divine assistance, for which we are encouraged to hope, relying on the mediation of Jesus Christ for the pardon of our manifold sins, and praying the God of all grace, through Him, to strengthen and enable us to keep this, our covenant, inviolate, and to establish and settle us, that at the second coming of Jesus, we may appear before his presence with exceeding joy."

As there can be no Episcopalian church without a *bishop*, so, I suppose, Mr. Editor, there can be no Congregational church without a *covenant*. This was certainly a rare specimen for the times. It is not for me to cavil with it. It was the remark of my father, that " Dr. Bancroft professed no more than he believed, and practised all he professed." " No man," said he, " ever identified himself with the interests of a place more closely than he did with those of the town of Worcester. He was always ready with a good word for every good work." And I incline to the belief that every old citizen of Worcester, holds to the same opinion that my father expressed; whether that good work was the education of the rising generation, the promotion of morality, or any public improvement. He lived beloved, and died — a few years ago — universally respected, by men of every variety of faith and worship. His wife was a daughter of John Chandler, a Judge of one of the courts.

My father was a great admirer of Gen. Washington, and was accustomed to speak often of what was done when Washington visited Worcester, the first year of his presidency; and I have heard him speak in glowing terms of a discriminating eulogy which Dr. Bancroft delivered in the Old South Church, at the request of the town, on the return of the anniversary of Washington's birthday, next after his decease. As he died on the 14th of December, 1799, the eulogy must have been delivered on the 22d of February, 1800. He had also a copy of a "Life of Washington," written by Dr. Bancroft, which he enjoined on me to read often, for the example it presented, and the excellent sentiments it inculcated.

The unassuming residence of the reverend guide of the second church, for so long a period, has seen a different race of occupants since he yielded to the inexorable demands of mortality. His study — where he read, and thought, and wrote — where so many pure aspirations went forth after that perfection which the Christian hopes for himself and for all — where he counselled with the afflicted, the old and the young — that study is now a place of daily trade, where segars and sugar candy, peppermints and peanuts, small beer and sundries are retailed, alike to the just and the unjust. It is a sad thought to me, that there was none of the "kith and kin," the parish or the priesthood, to save, even for a few short years, the good old man's hearthstone from such a desecration.

Yours,

CARL.

S

CHAPTER XVI.

Mr. Editor :—From an old newspaper, I learn that the first boy born in Worcester, was Adonijah Rice. There have been a great many boys born here since. His father was Jonas Rice, who came here, (the record says), in October, 1713, from the good town of Marlborough. Little Adonijah first opened his eyes, (again the record says), on the 7th of November, 1714, about 13 months after his father and mother took up their abode on Sagatabscot Hill, near the extensive meadows, that constitute a pleasant landscape, between the old roads leading to Grafton and Sutton. Now little Adonijah's father Jonas was undoubtedly a man of some education, and felt the importance, to the state, as well as to individuals, of giving his boy, and other boys, as good an education as the times and circumstances would permit; for I find that when little Adonijah had reached his twelfth year, the town employed his father, Jonas, in the capacity of a school teacher. They set him to work in April, and kept him employed until December, with such vacations only as were necessary to keep up the agricultural operations of the settlement. How good an education little Adonijah obtained, I do not know; for I find no mention of him after his birth, except that he served his country as a soldier, in the old French wars, and moved to Vermont, where he died an old man about the commencement of this century.

I fear that our forefathers did not engage in the business of education with so much zeal as they ought to have done; for it appears that little Adonijah's father Jonas did not "play the pedagogue" so much from choice as from necessity; for the town hired him "to teach such children and youth, as any of the inhabitants shall send to him, to read and write, *as the law directs.*" And I regret, Mr. Editor, that the truth of history requires me to state that the town did not set little Adonijah's father Jonas to work as a pedagogue until the grand jury had made a formal presentation of their negligence.

Twenty years ago, there stood a two-story wooden school house on the west side of Main street, nearly opposite the Bancroft house.* There was kept in it, at that time, a high school for girls, with two or three other schools of lower grades. At the same time there was a brick house on Thomas street, where there was a classical school, and also a high school for boys. Since that day, that house has been taken down, and rebuilt at the junction of Pine street with Pine Meadow road; and the large Thomas School house has been erected in its place. This new school house, denominated the Centre School house, was built on the lot next north of the old Centre house; and on account of the increase of business in Main street, has been nearly abandoned for school purposes; and before long will be given up wholly to the purposes of trade.

As we came to the Centre School house. my father said that he remembered well the first schools that were opened in that house. He said that after the War of the Revolution was over, old Gov. Lincoln, Dr. Dix, Dr. Green, and other prominent men of the town, joined together for the purpose of establishing

*Site of the Chadwick Building.

a school of a high order, and built the house on the front of the lot. Master Payson, he said, taught in the upper room what was called "The Seminary," an academy for the higher branches of education; and master Brown taught in the same building a school for the ordinary English branches. Both schools flourished finely for several years; both having occasionally public exhibitions, in the getting up of which there was a generous rivalry on the part of both pupils and teachers. But after about a dozen years of success, the school went down; the house was sold by auction, and bought up by the town or by the centre district. It was then moved to the back side of the lot, leaving a pleasant yard in front; and there the voices of many children rung often in my ears, until it was given up as a school house. It was sold not many years ago; was moved to the front of the lot, where it originally stood; and "another story built up at the bottom," as our gardener says of buildings that have been enlarged in that manner; so that where master Payson and master Brown once taught Latin and Greek, and mathematics, reading, writing and several of the 'ologies, there are now several stores at which may be bought teas and molasses, codfish and coffee; toy dolls and minature wagons, and penny whistles; and "laces so fine." [If there is any charge for this advertisement, I will pay the bill; for it is as much out of place in a newspaper communication, as was the remark of the good deacon in the conference meeting, when he said: — " I have no more doubt of the existence of a hell, than I have that there are one hundred barrels of flour in my store, which I will sell, to any one who wants to buy, at $6 the barrel for cash."]

" It is now about one hundred years ago," my father remarked, " that the town voted to erect a school house as near the centre of the south half of the town as it could be placed." Col. John Chandler undertook the task of locating the house. But there sprung up a controversy about his report which delayed the erection of the building for several years. It was settled at last by building the small house, spoken of in a former chapter of this tour, near the centre of Main street, in the vicinity of Lincoln Square.

Whether the patriot blacksmith of the Revolution, Col. Timothy Bigelow, received any portion of his education at this little seminary of learning by the roadside, I am not able to say ; as his family lived in the south part of the town, then known as Bogachoag, (now Auburn) ; but without doubt his wife, Miss Anna Andrews, the heiress, received at least a portion of her education there, as the school house was nearly opposite her father's residence. This humble school house, which was regarded of so much consequence to the town in its early days, was not given up until the "Seminary" came in to take its place.

How great the changes which are made in a century of progress ! Less than ninety years ago there were but four school districts in Worcester ; now there are fifteen, in which, as I am informed, from sixty to seventy teachers are employed. Of course there has been a corresponding increase in the machinery of education. Instead of the humble edifice of 1740, standing in front of the court house, 24 feet long, 16 feet wide, and with posts 7 feet high, and warmed and ventilated by a large open fire-place, the town has now several edifices devoted to educational purposes, which the "forefathers of the hamlet" would have pronounced "palaces of learning," if looking down the vista of time they could have seen the unpretending town of 1740 changed into the busy,

thrifty city of 1855, with its "palaces of art," where
industry accumulates wealth, and wealth supplies the
means of intellectual and moral culture and refine-
ment.   But, Mr. Editor, I must beg leave to express
my fears that a comparison of the expenses of education to-day with those of times long gone by, will
show that the present generation pays much higher for
what it gets, than was paid when Bigelow and others
received that education which fitted them to fill the
places they did fill with so much honor to themselves
and usefulness to the country.   I have a philosophy
of my own upon this subject ; but it is not the time to
broach it, farther than to say that in my view our
schools are, for young minds, too much like hot-beds
for young plants.   They grow large, but they do not
grow strong.   The boy Daniel Webster, among the
granite hills, attending the district schools less than
half of the year, and working upon the farm the rest
of the time, acquired a strength and vigor of mind,
which he would not have acquired shut up year after
year in a city school, where he gets but few of nature's glorious teachings, and where, as I have known
it to happen, the questions have been asked by boys,
big enough to know better, whether crows were not

sometimes white as well as black — and whether apple trees blossomed in spring or in autumn.

In this roving account of the Centre School House, I fear that I may have awakened the inquiry in some mind, whether I ever enjoyed the benefits of any school, either in town or country.

Yours,

CARL.

CHAPTER XVII

Mr. Editor :— As my father and myself, on our way south from the centre school house, came to the north corner of Central street, "that office (said he), was once occupied by my old friend Frank Blake;" and he gave me some account of the man, his life, his peculiarities, and his family connections.

Central street had at that time but two or three houses upon both sides of it. It was the principal road from Main street to the Canal basin, and the canal stores that stood around it. It was one of my early pleasures to go to the basin, and see the boats as they came up from Providence laden with flour, corn, salt, iron and other heavy articles, with now and then a family of prodigiously large wharf rats for passengers. As the colony is not yet extinct, I think they

came here as emigrants, and not as temporary visit-
ors. Chairs, chairs, everlasting in number, brought
into town in large loads from the northern parts of the
county, seemed to me to be the principal loading of
the boats down the canal. Had railroads never been
invented, the Blackstone Canal would, in time, have
done a large and profitable business. But the railroads took away its freight; the basin has been filled
up to accommodate railroads, foundries, etc.; and the
bridge and the store-houses have been superseded by
the progress of improvement. For a large portion of
the inhabitants of the Worcester of to-day a canal-boat
would be as much of a novelty as were the railroad
cars to the Worcester of twenty years ago, when on
the 4th of July, 1835, there was a grand celebration
of their running over the whole road from Boston to
Worcester.

Mr. Blake's office (then occupied by Hon. Isaac
Davis), with the house at the corner of Main and
Central streets, gave way, not long after my tour, to
the stone block that now occupies the ground on
which they stood. But I believe the office is still
standing in the rear, like one of those monuments of
the by-past, on which the friendly hand of some Old

Mortality must chisel anew the signs of past ownership, to save it from the common ashes of the things
that perish.

"Mr. Blake died nearly twenty years ago," said
my father, among the other remarks which he made
of him ; and I find by recurring to a brief memoir of
the man which was given to the public not long afterwards, that his death occurred on the 23d of February,
in the winter of the year 1817. He was the son of
merchant Joseph Blake, who moved from Boston to
our goodly town of Rutland, before the opening of the
Revolution, where he engaged largely in trade, and
where Francis, the fifth son, was born, (the record
says), October 14th, 1774. When Francis was five
years old, the family quitted the pleasant hills and
blue sky of Rutland, for the sand beach and blue
ocean of Hingham. One of the other four sons was
George Blake, of Boston, who for a long time filled
with distinguished ability the office of U. S. District
Attorney for Massachusetts ; and whom I have heard
my father speak of as one of the clearest and most forcible speakers that ever addressed a popular assembly,
and unsurpassed as a debater. There was talent in
the Blake family ; though I should judge that Francis

had more imagination than George, and was gifted
with a richer and loftier eloquence.

The college catalogue tells me that Francis Blake
graduated at the University in 1791 ; and I learn from
other sources that he was admitted to the bar in 1794,
and " put up his shingle" in Rutland, the place of
his nativity, where he remained till shortly after Mr.
Jefferson came into the presidency, in 1801.   His
brilliant talents attracted the notice of the Democrats
of Worcester and their admiration had been height-
ened by an oration which he delivered on the 4th of
July, 1796.   The two great parties, the Democrats
and Federalists, were then taking a distinct form in
the country ; so that on the succession of the Jefferson
administration to power, the Democrats felt compelled
to make no inconsiderable efforts to sustain themselves
against what they denominated " the slanders and the
libels of the Federalists" upon themselves and their
principles.   They determined to set up a democratic
press in Worcester, and liberal subscriptions for that
purpose, my father told me, were made by the senior
Gov. Lincoln, Gov. Sullivan, Gov. Eustis, " Honey"
Austin, as Benjamin Austin was called from some
pungent articles which he wrote under the signature

of "Honestus." They gave their newspaper the name of *The National Ægis;* and Francis Blake moved his office from Rutland to Worcester, and became its editor. My father had the early files of the paper, and many years afterwards he might often be seen, with his silver-bowed spectacles on, diligently perusing them as leisure gave him opportunity. The *Ægis* had "a hard row to hoe," so powerful were the prejudices of the community against the administration of Jefferson, and so influential were the appeals of the body of the clergy and others to put down the man who was represented as the tool and ally of the French Revolutionists. After conducting the *Ægis* three or four years, Mr. Blake dissolved his connection with it, and devoted himself to his profession. The paper passed through various fortunes, good, bad and indifferent; and at the time of which I am writing it was printed in the upper part of Green's block, in which at the time were the Central Bank, Harris's bookstore, and the offices of some of the principal lawyers of the town.

It was the remark of my father that nothing gave him more pleasure than to go into court, and hear Frank Blake in the arguments which he was often called to make in the cause of his numerous clients; he had always such a ready and rich eloquence, was so keen in drawing out and managing the testimony of witnesses, and had so much power over juries. Twice he represented Worcester county in the senate —just before the opening of the War of 1812. At the time of his death he was filling the office of clerk of the courts, to which he had been appointed but a short time before.

Several of the children, with the grandchildren, of this former distinguished citizen of Worcester, are now residents here; and walk the streets which he once walked; gaze upon the magnificient elms whose cooling shade he once enjoyed; survey the present landscape, the starry firmament, and the gorgeous sunsets, as he once did, from the hills that then surrounded the quiet hamlet, and on whose sides a busy population have erected tasteful residences that never entered into the dreams of the dwellers in the Worcester of forty years ago. I might have written more than I have written, of their distinguished relative; but if in what I have said, I have touched one memory or one sympathy with an unkindly hand, I hope they will pardon something to the spirit that would remind the generation of to-day of the virtues of the generations that have preceded them ; for I would impress upon all the poet's truth :

> " Men pass,
> Cleaving to things themselves which pass away,
> Like leaves on waves.   Thus all things pass forever,
> Save mind and the mind's meed."

Yours,

CARL.

CHAPTER XVIII.

Mr. Editor :— On the west side of Main street, facing into Central street, stood twenty years ago, as now, the residence of Dr. John Green, the third physician of that name in Worcester. It is a three-story brick house. My father remembered it when it was but two stories high, and Main street, in front of it, was at so great an elevation as to admit of passing from it into what is now a chamber window. It shows how great have been the changes in the grade of that street. I am not sure that he told me how long that place had been the residence of the Green family. He told me that the present occupant is the third of the name who have successively filled the post of physician to the people of Worcester. It struck me at the time as a remarkable fact to the history of a family, that it should afford three doctors of the same name in succession ; and, as opportunity has

9

occurred, I have from time to time minuted down, in the tablet of memory, such facts as I have been able to gather. For much of my information I am indebted to the Greens themselves, though they cannot tell who I am, nor the times when, nor the places where, I obtained my information.

The origin of the Green family in this region has about it an air of romance. Its founder, who was born in the first years of the 18th century came from Malden in Middlesex. It is said that the surgeon of a British ship was in the habit of visiting at his father's house in Malden; and that in the estimation of the boy Thomas, the British surgeon was a model man; and that the gift of a medical book, in those days when books were rarities, decided the future fate of the boy Thomas. He determined to be a doctor himself. At what time he left his father's house in Malden, I know not; but as the boy Thomas was about ten years old when little Adonijah Rice was born — the first birth in Worcester — I presume his exodus from Malden must have been shortly after the settlement of Jonas Rice in Worcester; a few years, more or less, making no essential difference when speaking of the minor events of the past.

I have no authority for this statement; but the supposition is my own, that the young man Thomas Green went out from his father's house, carrying with him his medical library of one volume, that he might associate with the Indians enough to obtain from them their secret of curing diseases; as in the early days of the country, medical men were glad to avail themselves of every means within their reach for enlarging their ability to heal the sick.   The young Dr. Thomas Green strolled away a two days' journey at least from the house of his childhood, till he came to a shelving rock that formed a sort of cave near a spring of pure water that bubbled out of " Strawberry Bank" — now Leicester Hill — where, like the modern philosopher of Walden Pond, he took up his abode; nature his teacher, the green earth his bed, the blue sky his covering, and the wild men of the forest his only neighbors.   There was something more than romance in that.   There was stern reality.   The medical philosopher became devout under the teachings of nature ; and as society gathered itself around him, the settlers looked to the man Thomas for medicine for the mind as well as medicine for the body.   He became a preacher as well as a doctor.   He gathered a church

— a Baptist church — and preached on Sundays and practised physic week days.

Time went on ; and when the preacher-doctor had reached nearly the middle point allotted as the life of man, there was born to him a son, whom he named John ; probably because it was the name borne by that disciple whom it is said " Jesus loved." The boy John was early initiated into the mysteries of the healing art, and as soon as he had reached his majority, he quitted the paternal roof at " Strawberry Bank ;" and following down the course of " Kettle Brook," he took up his abode in Worcester, nearly four score years anterior to the time when my father and I passed by the house of his worthy descendant.

This John the First, my father told me, married a daughter of the celebrated tory, Timothy Ruggles. You will remember the anecdote which my father told of him ; how that he was sitting as chief justice of the court of magistrates, for whom he entertained no very profound respect ; and that one day, when one of the chairs happened to be vacant, a large dog walked up and seated himself in the vacant chair, and how the brigadier judge, in a loud and peremptory voice, ordered the dog to get down out of the chair, and not presume to take that seat until he had been qualified by taking the oath of office. The brigadier judge was a man of mark ; and manifestly the blood of the Ruggleses has not yet run out. His daughter, the wife of John the First, was one of them in more senses than one. One of her sons yet lives among us ; and though I know but little of him beyond what I have heard from others, I doubt not that there is full as much of the Ruggles as of the Green in his composition. In wit and ready reply he is a fit representative of the brigadier judge. Hale and hearty he lives on the paternal estate upon the summit of a hill, that is reached by a narrow lane, at some distance to the northeast of Lincoln Square ; and when death calls for him, I doubt not he will be found, like Cooper's " Leather-Stocking," standing up six feet high, waiting for the summons, without a tear and without a fear.

My father was familiar with the whole history of the Greens. He used to speak often of John the First and his sons, and was intimate, I should think, with John the Second, whose sons, John the Third and his brothers, still live among us, a highly respected, though somewhat peculiar race. If I mistake not, the blood of Ruggles is in them all. What they will, they will; and·what they won't, they won't. But it is delicate ground on which I am treading, and I refuse to advance.

There was a Green, the son of the first John, of whom my father seemed to cherish recollections stronger than those of ordinary friendship. It was Timothy—named probably after his grandfather, or the brigadier judge. He was a lawyer, and opened an office at an early day in the city of New York. Business called him south just after the opening of the War of 1812. While at Charleston he was introduced to the family of Mr. Allston, the governor of South Carolina, whose wife was a daughter of the notable Aaron Burr. And in passing, I may remark that my father told me that he once saw Burr. It was not long before the time of which I am writing, that he was walking up Broadway, in company with a distinguished counsellor of the city of New York, when they met an old man, tottering around a corner, who seemed to have grown into the habit of shunning everybody, and being shunned by everybody. "That," said the counsellor to my father, "is the celebrated Aaron Burr; and he lives comparatively alone at such a house in that street." It was Timothy Green's introduction to the family of Gov. Allston that cost him his life. Mrs. Allston was desirous of visiting her father at New York; and as the land-route was too hard for her to travel, Timothy Green was induced to change his determination to return home by stages, and accompany Mrs. Allston by water. They took passage on board of a privateer for New York; and that was the last ever heard of them or the vessel. If they had been captured, it is probable that their fate would have become a matter of history. As they were never heard of more, it is more than probable that the ship was wrecked; and that all on board went down to sleep amidst the pearl and coral of the ocean, no more to be heard from till the sea shall give up the mighty multitude that, age after age, have sunk into its bosom, and over whom the wild waves are chanting a never-ceasing requiem. "Lost at sea" is the inscription on some branch of almost every family tree; and the Green family is not exempt from what seems the common calamity of the race.

Yours,

CARL.

CHAPTER XIX

Mr. Editor:—" Good day to you, Samuel!" said my father, as we came to the door of Burchstead's shoe-shop, in the basement of the four story brick house, next south of Dr. Green's. They shook hands and cracked jokes for a few minutes. "How is ' federal rib and cotton' to-day?" inquired my father. I do not remember the answer that was given; but I learned afterwards, that the smiling, witty, sarcastic individual, dressed in a large brown coat, whom my father addressed was old Mr. Samuel Brazer; and that the " federal rib and cotton" was a by-word between them, which had its origin more than forty years before; at the time when the " Green Store" was a factory, and when Mr. Brazer advertised and sold the corduroys and jeans manufactured there, under the expressive name of " federal rib and cotton."

In early life, Samuel Brazer opened a store in Worcester: but at what particular place, I have forgotten, if I ever knew. All I now remember, is that

my father told me that Mr. Brazer lost his dwelling-
house, his store, and most of his goods, in a disas-
trous fire which occurred nearly twenty years before,
one cold, snowy, stormy day in February, (1815),
when the house and bake-house of the late Elisha
Flagg, Esq., were also burnt to the ground. Mr.
Brazer's buildings had been replaced by the brick
house, already mentioned, and the two story wooden
building which was crushed by the falling walls of
Flagg Hall, which was destroyed by fire in the winter
of 1854. Mr. Flagg had replaced his with a double
three story brick house. and by one or more wooden
buildings south of it, which were moved away about
the time of my tour, to make room for the three story
brick building, in which for many years the Quinsigamond Bank was located. The house was taken
down to give place to Flagg Hall, and the bank
building shared the same fortune to give room for the
elegant and substantial four story block of six stores
that now covers the whole ground on which the
flames committed so much havoc with Mr. Flagg's
property in 1815, and again in 1854.

If I remember aright, it was the remark of my
father, that the late Wm. Lincoln, Esq., had an office

in the chambers of the wooden building which occupied the ground where the south end of Flagg's Block
now stands; and that there he practised law, edited
the *Ægis*, and wrote those famous "pig reports" for
the agricultural fairs, that were so extensively published and commended for their wit and humor.

Mr. Brazer, at the time of which I am writing,
had retired from business; and although far advanced
in life, he was "ripe for fun," at all times, and at the
expense of himself or his friends. It was remarked
by my father, that Mr. Brazer loved a "cut" upon
his minister, the Rev. Dr. Bancroft, as much as upon
any one of his acquaintance; and I remember of his
telling of a passage between them, in which Mr.
Brazer unbridled his sarcasm at the doctor's expense.
The doctor was telling a company how he was preaching once by candlelight, when his notes caught fire
and it was with difficulty that he saved his sermon.
"Why didn't you let it burn?" inquired Brazer;
"your audience would have got more light from it
in that way than in any other!"

Mr. Brazer had two sons; both of whom, I have
heard my father remark, were "chips of the old
block." Their names were Samuel and John. He

tried to make a merchant of Samuel, by putting him
in a store in Boston; but as he could not succeed in
inspiring him with any love for that employment, he
took him home, to fit him for a profession, with the
hope, he was accustomed to say, that "he might get
his living by his wits, if he couldn't by good hits."
He must have been a young man of rare abilities;
but with a certain obliquity of mind that prevented
him from rightly appreciating the purpose of life and
its duties. He learned his lessons too easily to be
a close, persevering student; and his love of fun frequently led him into little "scrapes," which, though
free from malice, were nevertheless hindrances to
success. He was fitted for college; but never went
there. He studied law; but never loved his profession. Newspaper columns for him had many attrac-
tions; and in the early columns of the *Ægis*, were
many sharp articles, both of prose and poetry, which
my father used to read over, with a relish, accompa-
nying them with the remark, "That's one of Sam's!"
His feelings were too genial for success in the cold
ploddings of professional life. He loved the excitement of momentary success; and therefore after a temporary occupancy of a law office in some small town

in our county of Franklin, with little or no business,
he came back to Worcester, and assumed the duties
of editor of the *Ægis*. I think it was not long
afterward, that he quitted Worcester, went to Balti-
more, and became the editor of the *Patriot*, published
in that city. "Sam was a downright clever fellow,"
said my father; "I missed him much when he left
us; and heard of his death with much sorrow."

The other son of Samuel Brazer, Rev. John Brazer, D. D., a clergyman in Salem until his death
within a few years, was probably known to most of
your readers by reputation, if not personally. He
had the family characteristics; but they were in sub-
jection to high and pure motives. He graduated at
Harvard College with high honor as a scholar; immediately became one of its tutors, and subsequently a
professor; and in a few years dissolved his connection
with the college, and was ordained as a preacher over
a leading Unitarian society in Salem. It was always
a pleasure to me to hear him preach, as occasionally I
did; for from the pulpit then,

> "A voice arose,
> Solemn and sweet as when low winds attune,
> The midnight pines."

The east side of Main street, opposite Brazer's and Flagg's buildings, has now nothing upon it that was there twenty years ago. A dwelling house and a law office were shoved away, a few years since, to make room for the "Waldo Block;" and last year the old Central Hotel was cut into quarters, and on the ground has since arisen an elegant four story hotel,* in modern style, which from present indications, the public will soon be invited to occupy. I know not how long it had been a public house; but if my memory serves me, my father told me that a part of it was once the house of Dea. Daniel Heywood; and shortly after the incorporation of Worcester county one of the chambers was used for the county jail. Several additions have been made from time to time; and within my own recollection an elegant portico — one of the best specimens of architectural taste in town — was erected over the entrance. How it came to be there, I know not; but I always loved the sight of it, and regretted the loss of it. The house was once kept by Mr. Hathaway : but that was before my day, and I should not have known it, had I not heard my father make the remark that "Hathaway was a prince among landlords."

*The Bay State House.

As we passed it on our way to the Common, we saw the people very busy in their preparations for the "Cattle Show Ball," that was to "come off" there that evening; for at that time the hall of the Central Hotel was the only public hall in Worcester, except the old town hall; and it was used on all occasions. There was no other ball room in town, no other suitable place where the "light fantastic toe" could agitate itself to its owner's satisfaction. We came to a knot of young gentleman who were in hot disputation over the grave and solemn matter of an invitation which one of the managers had had the temerity to extend to an individual, who it was said, was "nothing but a mechanic," and therefore not entitled to social position among those who then claimed the exclusive right to control an agricultural ball. The illiberal spirit, then manifested, found it difficult to sustain its petty exclusiveness. It has melted down to nothing, or so near to nothing as to be insignificant in its demonstrations.

Yours,

CARL.

CHAPTER XX.

Mr. Editor :—"Columbian Avenue," said my father, "is the magnificent name which they have given to this narrow road." It is now Exchange street.* It had been opened but a short time, I believe, from Main to Summer streets, with a rickety wooden bridge where there is now one of stone, across what was then the Blackstone Canal. It is now lined with buildings on both sides, and a portion of the street was the centre of the very destructive fire of June, 1854. At the time of which I am writing, stood a two story brick building, then occupied as a dry goods store. The owner and his lady stood in the door. "They say he keeps his wife to hang dry goods on," was the remark of my father; "but I think it is a slander, for she is a smart as well as pretty woman." At the distance of a few feet south, on Main street, stood the Bank Building. It was an L

*At one time called Market Street.

block of three stories, and was built about the beginning of the present century by the Worcester Bank;
one part of it for banking purposes, and the other
for the house of its president, the late Mr. Waldo,
who lived there, my father remarked, until an individual, with none of the best of motives, obstructed
the light and air of the windows by erecting the store,
of which I have just spoken. Mr. Waldo had then
built him a new house, on the lot next south; and
the bank building, with the exception of the banking-
rooms, was then the fashionable boarding-house of
the town. It shortly afterwards became the "Central
Exchange;" and in it were the post-office, several
law offices, and printing offices. The store became
the "York House," and was occupied as a victualling
house; to which a high brick building had been
added as a wool store. It was a cold Sunday night,
a few years afterwards, in which I was aroused by
an alarm of fire; and running with speed to the
scene, I was pained to find the "York House" envel-
oped in fire, and the flames pouring from its roof into
all the north windows of the Central Exchange. But
I have no occasion, Mr. Editor, to recall the scene to
your mind, inasmuch as your *Palladium* went down

in the deluge of fire. But you know not the regrets
I experienced at my apprehension that I might suffer
the loss of my weekly visitor, which had even then
become one of my necessities; nor the gratification
which I experienced, when two days after, the paper
appeared as usual, furnishing the history of its own
death and resurrection.

My father showed me an ancient pear tree that
stood in the vicinity of the Exchange; and told me
that it was more than a hundred years old; that it was
planted by Dea. Daniel Heywood, one of the early
settlers, who owned land upon that portion of the east
side of Main street; and on which, near the Exchange, there was erected the second garrison in
Worcester — the first one having been established at a
point which he showed me on the rising ground west
of the head of Park street. Subsequently Dea. Heywood built him a house, near the spot, which afterwards became a part of the late Central Hotel.

This Dea. Heywood was evidently a man to make
a mark in whatever he attempted. He was a man of
a positive, and not of a negative, character. He
belonged to the party that made the first permanent
settlement in Worcester. He was a good Christian,

10

and a good soldier, who could use both "spiritual
and carnal weapons" with equal adroitness, I infer
from such facts in relation to him as have come down
to the present time. He took an active part in establishing the first church in town, and was honored
with the post of its first deacon ; and in those days the
office of a deacon was one of high honor, and as much
coveted as is that of postmaster or tidewaiter at this
day. He was probably conscientious in the movement, and justified himself by an argument upon the
necessity of the case, but I can but regret that he
should have encouraged, as I have reason to believe
he did — even if he did not take a part in it — the
destruction of the meeting-house of the " Scotch Cov-
enanters," while they were building it in the high
grounds of Lincoln street. But the good deacon
probably believed that it was his duty to fight as well
as to pray : for it appears that he was ever ready to
observe the "wholesome law" of the old colonial
legislature, which required that every man should go
to church and carry his gun and half a dozen ball
cartridges ; but forbid them, under a penalty of five
shillings for each offence, to fire off a gun on Sunday,
" at any game whatsoever, *except an Indian* or a

wolf." And Dea. Heywood, I said, was a good soldier, as well as a good Christian : for I find that when he was some thirty years older than he was when he was chosen deacon, he took command of a company — a full one of soldiers enlisted in Worcester, who made a part of Gen. Dwight's command in an expedition against the Indians. History tells me that it was on the 8th day of August, 1748,— one hundred and seven years ago,— that fifty-three volunteer soldiers, citizens of Worcester, paraded in Main street, opposite the Central Exchange : and that *Major* Heywood, acting as captain, came from his house, and took command of them : and that after reviewing them, in the presence of a large portion of the inhabitants of the town, and finding them "armed and equipped as the law directs," he marched them off to join the main body of Dwight's troops, in their determination to slay the Indians, or drive them off to Canada. The French were in possession of Canada, and they instigated the Indians to annoy the American settlements. But as good luck would have it deacon-major and his men came back safe, after an absence of about three weeks among the granite hills, not having had a chance to spend any of their ammuni-

tion on any such "game" as Indians.   In this they
were fortunate.   The Indians kept out of their reach.
They were less powerful at that day than they were
when the Nipmuck tribe reigned supreme in all this
region, making their headquarters on Pakachoag Hill,
where now stands the College of the Holy Cross ; and
hunting upon these hills, and fishing in Quinsigamond and other ponds and streams.

   Heywood and his associates must have been men
of iron nerves and resolute wills.   Two companies of
settlers had preceded them, and failed in their purpose
of effecting a settlement.   They were constantly ex-
posed, and often seriously annoyed by the Indians
who skulked about in the vicinity.   He came here
from Concord in Middlesex ; and besides being the
the first in the long line of deacons in Worcester, he
was for a good many years chairman of the board of
selectmen ; though I think he was not a member of
the first board that was chosen after the incorporation
of the town in 1722.   He was also treasurer and town
clerk, and took a leading part in town business.

   There was another Heywood, who, subsequently,
was one of the most distinguished men of Worcester.
I am not certain of the fact, but it is my impression

that he was a nephew of the deacon: and that his father came from Concord with him, and afterwards crossed Quinsigamond. and located himself on the east side in Shrewsbury. This was Judge Heywood, whose descendants are among us to-day. Benjamin was his name. He served an apprenticeship as a carpenter: but subsequently went to college: and when the War of the Revolution broke out, he joined the army as a lieutenant: was soon made a captain and subsequently a paymaster. He served through the war, and enjoyed in an eminent degree, the confidence and esteem of officers and soldiers. For a period of some ten years near the commencement of the present century he was a judge of the court of common pleas: and during his life he filled other important positions assigned him by the government or the people.

It is said that the biggest individuals that walk upon the face of the earth, are boys from sixteen to twenty years of age: that they know a vast deal more than they ever know at any later period of their lives; and I have a suspicion that they never fully outgrow the feeling: for I find that some of the present generation seem to be afflicted with the idea that Worcester was not much of a place before they came upon its stage of action ; and that there would be great uncertainty as to its fate if they should chance to be called away.   But admitting all the consequence which they attach to themselves, I can not avoid the impression that Worcester has had some men of influence and character in every period of its existence as a municipal body.

Yours,

CARL.

CHAPTER XXI.

Mr. Editor :—The building which was so long occupied by the Worcester Bank—afterwards the old Central Exchange—was erected, my father remarked, by the late Col. Peter Kendall ; and the bricks, which were large and handsome, were carted into town from Sterling. An accident, he also remarked, happened there to our townsman, William Harrington, which resulted in the loss of one of his limbs. That must have been as much as fifty years ago. The bank has been in operation fifty-one years, and has had but three presidents all the while. At the time of its incorporation there were but few banks in the State. Its capital was a large one for a country bank at that time—$200,000. Its first president was Daniel Waldo, senior : its second, Daniel Waldo, the younger, who filled the office for more than forty years ; and its third, the present incumbent, Hon. Stephen Salisbury. Either of its presidents could have owned the whole stock well enough, if they had chosen to do so. Of Daniel Waldo, the elder, you remember, I have already related an anecdote told me by my father, how he was sent for by the Shays men, in the time of the rebellion, and marched through the street, by a file of soldiers, to the " Hancock Arms," to answer to the grave charge of poisoning the sugar which the soldiers mixed with their rum; and how he was discharged upon the discovery that the poison which so seriously alarmed those who had taken it, proved to be *snuff*, which Mr. Waldo's clerk had accidentally dropped into the sugar; and how they were reconciled by the gift of a keg of West India rum. My father knew the elder Waldo. He said that he moved from Boston to Worcester while the War of the Revolution was in progress; and that so far as he remembered,—for he was but a lad then,—Mr. Waldo's sympathies were with the tory side. He was spoken of also, by the people of that day, as " aristocratic " in his tastes and habits; and there were many caustic remarks made upon his extravagance in owning a one-horse chaise. I suppose from that circumstance that there was no

other one in town at that time. It was then the
universal custom for a gentleman and lady, when
going to church or elsewhere, to ride horseback—the
lady upon a pillion behind the gentleman's saddle.
The young folks walked : and they were prudent then,
for I have heard my father say, that many was the
time that he had seen the young ladies who lived out
of the village, put on shoes and stockings when they
came in sight of the meeting-house, and take them off
again when going home, walking bare-foot to save
shoe-leather. Young ladies were more robust and
hardy then : still I think the young ladies of to-day
may save their constitutions without a literal imitation
of a custom which was considered praiseworthy in
their grandmothers.

Many of our young readers, I doubt not, will be
interested in the statement that banking business was
a different matter with the Worcester Bank, in its
early years, from what it is now. The notes discounted
were signed, jointly and severally, by two or more
individuals, and made payable in sixty days. At the
end of that period, an instalment on the note was paid
to the bank, of ten or twenty per cent. as previously
agreed upon, with the interest on the amount remaining

unpaid, for another period of sixty days; and this process was repeated every sixty days until the whole loan was repaid. But the note could be put in suit at any time after the expiration of the first sixty days.

So high was the character of the " Worcester Bank," that its bills always circulated (I have been told), as readily in the West and South as the bills of any other New England bank. I have heard of an item of its history which produced great excitement in its day. It must have been nearly or quite thirty years ago, at the time what used to be called the " Suffolk Bank System" went into operation. It had previously been the custom for the banks in Boston to send out messengers to the country banks, with the bills which they had taken on those banks, and get the specie for them, which they carted off to Boston. The Suffolk Bank introduced the plan of requiring the country banks to make a deposit in Boston for the redemption of their notes there. The Worcester Bank did not accede to the arrangement: and the Suffolk picked up all its notes it could find, and then made a " run " on the Worcester for their redemption. It did not succeed in *forcing* the Worcester into its plan; which was afterwards voluntarily adopted.

You will allow me in this connection to relate an anecdote I have heard of a cashier of a country bank. A run was made upon him for a greater amount than he had specie in his vault.   It was afternoon ; and he proceeded very deliberately in opening and counting out package after package, until the clock struck a certain hour.   Then stopping he said :   "We never do business after this time of day, and we will stop where we are."   The messenger demurred, and insisted upon going through with the job, so that he could return to Boston.   But the cashier was immovable.   Not another dollar would he count that day to please anybody.   The messenger insisted upon their remaining in the bank.   "Very well (said the cashier). if you choose to remain you can ; I am going out, and shall lock you in."   Not liking the prospect of a night's imprisonment, the messenger most unwillingly postponed his departure till the next day.   In the meantime the cashier rode post-haste to the nearest bank he could find ; borrowed specie enough to accommodate the Boston gentleman with the sum he was after ; and opened his bank in the morning at the usual hour, and with a smiling face took up the business where they left it the day before.   So much for regular hours of business and the benefits of a strict adherence to them.   Had he kept his bank open beyond the customary hour, the day he was called upon, it would have failed as sure as fate before sunset.   *Mem.*   Cashiers should take time to count their money very carefully, when they are short of specie funds.

At the time of which I write, Daniel Waldo, the younger — the second president of the Worcester Bank — resided with three sisters in the three-story brick house next south of the bank building.   Neither of them were ever married.   They had one of the largest estates ever held in the interior of the State : and I doubt not that less charitable dispositions than they possessed would have made their accumulations of wealth vastly greater than they were.   The elder Gov. Lincoln married another sister.   The late Mr. Waldo was scrupulously exact in all his transactions.   He was the financier of the family.   His liberality was evinced on many occasions, though not in any broad sweep.   And by his will the mass of his property was bestowed upon missionary and other societies.   It was with regret that I heard that he gave nothing comparatively to the town where his life was passed, and in which his money was made ; for had he done so his name would have been cherished through ages as a public benefactor.   As it is, I fear it will nowhere be found, a few years hence, except upon some inconsiderable building or street.   Even his mansion house has already fallen a victim to the spirit of progress, and been shoved down to a new street across the foot of his garden : and on its site the Mechanics' Hall is now rising, to bury beneath its importance every association connected with the former occupancy of the land.

Mr. Waldo was modest and unobtrusive in his deportment.   He belonged to the old federal party in politics, and was a member of the notable convention which met at Hartford during the War of 1812.   He was a good man, and a useful and much-respected citizen : and might, if he had chosen to do so, have shared largely in those substantial honors, which are too often won in the arena of politics at the sacrifice of the solid and enduring happiness of private life. It is true that his property was his own, to dispose of as suited his pleasure : but I could have wished that with a portion of it some monument might have been reared that would have sent his name, " sparkling down to the tide of time," as a great public benefactor to the community in which he lived, connected with some department of literature, science, or art, of industry, or of philanthropy in some of the various forms it assumes for the benefit of mankind.

Of the cashiers of the Worcester Bank, Levi Thaxter, Esq., was the first. How long he served in that capacity, I know not: but I believe that its late cashier, our respected citizen Samuel Jennison, Esq., filled the office for a period of at least thirty years. For at least half of that time he was also the treasurer of the Worcester County Institution for Savings, and transacted all the business of that institution in connection with the bank, with the aid of occasional clerk-hire. The Savings Bank, I find, went into operation in 1828. At the end of the first year its deposits amounted to only about $6000. At the end of eight years, they had risen to about $276,000. From that time the increase was rapid; and they now amount to not less than $1,800,000: and in the mean time the Mechanics Savings Bank has come into being, and has now an amount of deposits considerably larger than the old institution had in 1836.

For a period of twenty-four years, the Worcester Bank was the only banking institution in town. New men and new interests have come forward to be accommodated, until there are now six banks, instead of one, with an aggregate capital of nearly a million and a half.

Yours.

CARL.

CHAPTER XXII.

Mr. Editor : — Next south of the Waldo house, stood a three story frame house, with a one story L facing Main street, which was moved away a few years ago, to give place to the spacious and elegant four story Union Block. I noticed the small sign of "Post Office" over the door. My father stepped into a small entry — perhaps six feet square, with a few letter boxes in front, and a delivery window at one side. "How do you do, deacon?" said he : "have you anything in the office for me to-day?" In a moment I heard the quick and rather sharp reply, from an elderly man inside : "*Nothing at present.*"

The individual thus addressed was Deacon James Wilson, the postmaster. He was of middling size, and dressed somewhat in the style of a gentleman of the old school ; with a long, large coat, long, slashed vest; breeches, long stockings, shoes, knee buckles, and shoe buckles. "He is not always the most civil of men," was the remark of my father; "and I suppose his long and constant confinement makes him a little petulant at times." I remember that he said also that the deacon did all the business of the post-office himself; his daughter taking his place in his absence. Such was the Worcester post-office but little more than twenty years ago. In a former chapter of this history, you will remember that I said that the first postmaster here was the celebrated Isaiah Thomas. I think he had his appointment from Benjamin Franklin. Mr. Thomas moved the Spy printing office from Boston to Worcester in the spring of 1775. If I remember rightly, my father said it was opened in a small building on Lincoln Street, near the "Hancock Arms." In the following autumn, Mr. Thomas was appointed postmaster, and had the post-office for a time at the same place; but subsequently moved it to "Court Hill." I am not able to state it as a positive fact, but I have the impression that Mr. Thomas retained the post-office until the accession of Mr. Jefferson to the presidency in 1801; when, in the general sweep that followed, he was either removed, or not

11

reappointed, and the office was given to Deacon Wilson. He held it from 1801 to near the close of 1833 —a period of 32 years—when he was removed, and Jubal Harrington, Esq., was appointed by Amos Kendall, Gen. Jackson's efficient postmaster-general. I remember that there was a good deal of violent denunciation of Gen. Jackson about town because of the deacon's removal. Even the good deacon himself did not manifest a spirit of resignation; but shut up his door, and refused to let the office remain on his premises for a single day. Mr. Harrington took a room in the Exchange Coffee House, where the office was kept until it was removed to the old Central Exchange. In the winter of 1839 the office became vacant, and M. L. Fisher, Esq., received from Mr. Van Buren the appointment of postmaster. Four years afterwards, as I have before stated, the Exchange was destroyed by fire. The contents of the post-office, I am told, were all saved; and the next morning the letters and mails were delivered from the law office of Hon. Isaac Davis. In a day or two it was removed to a low building which had been occupied as a "stage office," at the corner of Main and Mechanic streets; and was continued there until the commencement of

the following winter, when the new Central Exchange
was completed.

My father was accustomed to speak of Deacon
Wilson as "a precise body," who, I should think was
rather set in his own ways, and somewhat rigid in his
notions.   He was an Englishman, who came to this
country from the north of England near the close of
the last century ; and must have been appointed postmaster very shortly after taking his naturalization
papers as an American citizen.   In his religious views
and associations he was a Baptist ; and my father was
accustomed to make the remark that " Dea. Wilson
was the father of all the Baptists in Worcester."   I do
not think that his remark implied anything more than
that he was one of the first of that denomination in
town, and was largely instrumental in building it up.
Indeed I have since been informed that at the time
Deacon Wilson came here to live there was but one
Baptist in town—the first Dr. John Green, who was
the son of the preacher doctor, Thomas Green, of
whom I have before written as the first preacher and
doctor in the town of Leicester.

Deacon Wilson, as my father remarked, held meetings in his own house for a good many years, until

the breaking out of the War of 1812, when the pastor of the Old South Church, Rev. Dr. Austin, gave " mortal offence" to the democrats by a sermon which he preached upon the war, and in which he handled Mr. Madison and the war party without clerical mittens. Such members of his church as were democrats then left his meeting in large numbers, and united with Deacon Wilson in organizing the First Baptist Church. They took the hall in · the old Centre School House for meetings on Sabbath, and proceeded in the erection of a small meeting house east of the Common, where the First Baptist meeting house now stands. As the society increased in numbers, it was found necessary to enlarge the house by adding wings to each side. But I find by recurring to the annals of the day, that it was on a mild night about the 20th of May in the year 1836, that some " peacemaker" effected a "compromise" of a controversy that had sprung up in the parish about the meeting house, by applying to it the torch of the incendiary, and in a short time the whole was a mass of ruins. The way was thus cleared for the erection of a new house on the same spot, whose steeple I have often heard commended by strangers as one of the best specimens of architecture in Worcester.

Deacon Wilson was chosen the first deacon of the
Baptist Church at the time of its organization, and
held the place until his removal from the post-office,
when, if my memory serves me, he left Worcester,
and took up his residence in one of the western states.
I never hear the remark, " Nothing at present," as I
sometimes do, but it brings up before me the form
and figure of the ancient postmaster, as his voice first
struck my ear on that pleasant autumnal day when in
company with my father I made my tour through
Main street. Could he return and visit anew the
place where he so long resided, wonderful would he
find the changes that have occurred in the comparatively brief period of twenty years. His house with
its little post-office attached has gone from its foundations, and "nothing at present" indicates where it
once stood. The church which he labored so hard to
establish, and over whose infancy he watched with
parental solicitude, has "swarmed," as they say of
bees, once and again ; the second church having been
formed many years ago, and been long in strong occupancy of a house of worship on Pleasant street ; and
the third having been some time organized, and now
building an elegant and substantial meeting house of
brick, at a point in Main street which twenty years

ago was "quite out of town." Instead of a post-office with a handful of letters each day, which one person could manage, he would find letters coming in by the bushel, and a half a dozen clerks and penny posts to deliver them. He would be convinced that in this age of steam, and electricity, and wind, and bustle, things go on as with a destiny which man is feeble to control or direct. If he did not believe in "spiritualism," or "animal magnetism," I think he would adopt the conclusion that there is in these days a good deal of *material magnetism*, which operates with great force in bringing wood, and stone, and bricks, and iron, together in large masses, and moulding and shaping them into elegant and costly edifices, that are either the temples where industry worships mammon, or the homes of a happy and refined civilization.

Yours,

CARL.

CHAPTER XXIII

Mr. Editor:—Next south of Deacon Wilson's little post-office, stood, twenty years ago, the residence of the late Hon. Samuel M. Burnside ; next to that a one story wooden building, occupied by Mr. Burnside, and the late Hon. Alfred Dwight Foster, as their law office ; and next south, the house of Mr. Foster. There was a fence in front, and yards with shrubbery. All these buildings were given up, not long afterwards, to the purposes of trade, except Mr. Foster's house, to which another story was added, and other extensive additions made ; and it has since rendered the public good service as the "American House."*

An accident, which it is of no importance to your readers to know, made me acquainted early with Mr. Burnside ; and that acquaintance, which was always

---

*This stood on the north corner of Foster street.

valuable to me, continued without interruption to his death, which I sincerely lamented.   He was a man of a strongly marked character, and many peculiarities, which many people misinterpreted, because they did not read him aright.   He was an honest man in his sentiments and in his dealings.   I was standing once in the post-office entry with my father, who was conversing with the postmaster.   Mr. Burnside came in, and took his letters from the office, and walked away. In a few minutes, he came back walking rapidly, and said to the postmaster :—" This is a *double* letter, and I have paid only *single* postage upon it ; " at the same time handing to the postmaster another postage.   How few are the men who would have done that !   Yet the postmaster told my father that Mr. Burnside had done it hundreds of times—always coming back with the additional postage after he had opened the letter, and discovered that it was undercharged.

Mr. Burnside read much ; not the law only, but general literature, the news of the day, and especially works on theology.   His mind was active and inquiring. It was often that I heard him speak in private ; but very seldom in public ; yet when he did speak in public, he spoke to the point, with plainness and directness, and in a style of elegance that is seldom attained by public speakers. No man used better language than he for the communication of his ideas.

Mr. Burnside was of Scotch descent; his ancestors being of that colony that left Scotland about two centuries ago, and settled in the northern part of Ireland, in County Londonderry, I believe; from which they subsequently emigrated to America. In that same company came the Irish James Rankin, of whom I have before spoken as the father of the beautiful Anna Rankin, who married the young collegian Sam. Andrews; whose daughter, Anna Andrews, was the wife of the patriotic blacksmith, Col. Timothy Bigelow. I believe that Mr. Burnside's ancestors were of the Scotch-Irish who first settled Londonderry in New Hampshire; and he once told me of the perils which his father met with as an early settler on the banks of the Connecticut, in the Upper Coös. He was liberally educated, and a well read lawyer; and no man took a deeper interest than he did in public education. It was but recently that I heard awarded to him, by one who seemed to know, the high honor of being the author of the law which our legislature passed nearly thirty years ago, that gave the first

impulse to our modern system of common school
education. After giving up his house and office on
Main street, he built himself a large and handsome
residence upon the high grounds of Chestnut street,
west of Main street, where he enjoyed till his death,
a few years ago, the affluence he had accumulated.
If there is any merit in the commendation I have
bestowed upon Mr. Burnside as a man and a citizen,
it is because it is an entirely disinterested commendation.

Opposite the residence of Mr. Burnside, at the time
of which I am writing, at a considerable elevation
above Main street, stood the Maccarty house. It was
moved back upon a cross street in the rear, not long
afterwards, and now stands near the Classical and
English High School. At the southeast corner of the
lot, where is now the entrance into Maple street, there
was one of the ancient stores of the town. My father
gave me its history; but it has unfortunately fled from
me. The house and the store were removed to make
room for the Brinley Block, for the erection of which
with its beautiful Hall, Worcester was indebted, nearly
twenty years ago, to the enterprise of our fellow citizen, Benjamin Butman. Esq. The utilitarian spirit

got possession of the hall a few years ago, and somewhat marred its architectural effect by substituting iron
posts for its elegant wooden columns.

The Maccarty house, at the time of which I am
speaking, was occupied by the widow of Nathaniel
Maccarty, who died but a few years before.   He was
the twelfth child of the Rev. Nathaniel Maccarty, the
third minister settled in Worcester.   My father remembered the minister, and spoke of him as he appeared to him in his youth—a tall, spare man, with
dark complexion, and large, bright eyes, too old or too
feeble to preach often.   He had been settled here at
that time between thirty and forty years ; and was evidently a preacher of a good deal of ability and influence.
Rev. Mr. Maccarty's wife was the daughter of a Welsh-
man, who was a wealthy merchant in Boston, by the
name of Gatcomb.   They lived at the parsonage,
which stood south of the Common, on what is now
Park street ; and they had the poor minister's fortune,
a small salary and a large family ; she having been
the mother of four daughters, and eleven sons, several
of whom died in their infancy. Nathaniel, whose residence was where Brinley Hall* now stands. was the

*Now called Grand Army Hall.

tenth son.   In youth he was apprenticed to Isaiah
Thomas, to learn the trade of a printer; and while in
the employ of Mr. Thomas, he was sent out, once in
each week, as a postrider, from Worcester, to carry
newspapers and letters into the towns in the northerly
part of Worcester county.   Whether he learned the
trade of a printer, or not, I am unable to say; but I
remember to have heard my father say that he made a
fortune in trade, in some country town I think it was
Petersham—and came back to Worcester to enjoy it in
the quiet town of his nativity.   I had no personal
knowledge of the man, nor any recollection of him.

As we passed the house, a young lawyer by the
name of G—— F—— now of New York—came out of
the gate.   My father spoke with him; and Mr. F——
told him that he slept in the house because the old
lady had become very much excited and alarmed by an
anonymous letter she had received, from some unknown
individual, threatening to murder her if she did not
send a large sum of money to the writer.   It was not
long after the murder of old Mr. White of Salem, which
produced an intense sensation in all this section of the
country, and which made us young folks tremble in
our beds whenever the wind rattled a blind upon our

house. Mr. F—— told my father who he thought was the writer of the letter; and my father asked me if I heard the name; and upon my answering in the affirmative, he said I must never lisp it to any person, if I did, perhaps the writer of the letter would murder me. I have faithfully kept the secret to this day; and never have I seen that individual about town, from that time to this, but I have felt towards him the same aversion which the eccentric John Randolph entertained towards a harmless portion of the brute creation, when he said: "I would go forty rods any time to kick a sheep."

Mr. Maccarty, by his will, left a small sum of money—I think it was $500—the interest of which was to be spent in setting out trees and ornamenting the grounds of the State Lunatic Hospital, which was erected here about the time of his death.

With the late Mr. Foster, my acquaintance never went beyond that of an inconsiderable recognition. His father, I have understood, was a man of note, and lived in Brookfield when that town was a place of more notoriety than Worcester. I find his name among the men who represented Massachusetts in congress when John Adams was president of the

United States. The late Mr. Foster was educated for the profession of the law ; but other objects seemed to engross his attention. He was one of the founders of Union Church, and contributed liberally of his wealth towards the erection of the meeting house, and the support of the ministry. I remember him as the first president of the Quinsigamond Bank, and for several years as a trustee and treasurer of the State Lunatic Hospital ; and also as a representative and senator in the general court, and one of the governor's councillors. In whatever contributed to the advancement of popular education, he seemed to take more than a casual interest, both as a citizen and a member of the school committee. Yet it is an opinion that I can not withhold, that if he had been dependent for a living upon his own efforts, he had the ability to take a high rank and make his mark in his profession. But in surrendering his law office, and retiring to the quiet of private life, he became too much cut off from the actualities of life for society to receive, what it might otherwise have received, the benefits of his calm judgment, high sense of right, and liberal views of what every man owes to his fellow men.

Yours,

CARL.

CHAPTER XXIV

Mr. Editor: — I think it was in 1831 that the legislature incorporated the Boston & Worcester Railroad Company : and at the time of which I am writing, the road was in process of construction. The cars were running on the easterly end; and it was there that the trial was made of the first locomotive engine used on any railroad in this country. All manner of sneering remarks were made about the " tea-kettle on a firecart." It being in my boy days, I remember well what was said of the experiment. No one expected that it could be used except at those seasons of the year when the rails might be clear of snow ; and it was the remark of my father, once when we were looking at an engine, that the projectors of the road had no conception, at the time they took their charter, that they could run their cars in any other manner than by horse-power ; and he said farther, that when they were getting the project under way, they proposed that every man, who chose, should have the right to go upon the railroad with his own horse and wagon, fitted to the track, under the direction of its managers.

The building of this railroad was a marvel to the inhabitants all along the line. Previously they had considered a short cut through a hill, for a public highway, as a great curiosity to be visited ; and therefore their surprise was great when they saw them cutting down hills and filling up valleys, without regard to height or depth, and with no apparent consideration except the straightest line from one point to another. The road was not then open to Worcester. It was delayed by the deep rock cutting, in the easterly part of the town, which is the backbone of the road ; but it was staked out to come up to Main street in front of the house of Mr. Lincoln, then, as for several years previously, the excellent governor of the commonwealth ; and for its purposes the company purchased the house of the late John W. Stiles. Esq., with his garden in the rear. The house was removed not many years ago, and the Universalist Church erected upon the spot.*

---

*The old Universalist Church building of wood still remains on the corner of Main and Foster streets. The audience room is known as Continental Hall.

Gov. Lincoln's was a three story brick house, with a large yard in front, filled with trees, and shrubs, and flowers. To my youthful vision, it was a delightful residence : such as any man might rejoice to own and occupy, and regret to leave. It was but a short time afterwards that I passed that way again, and saw that it had been touched by the spirit of progress. The governor with his men was at work cutting out and making up what is now Elm street. There is now a church* on the spot, or near to it, where his barn then stood : and the land in the rear were hay-fields and corn fields, where are now handsome streets and elegant houses. The mansion itself, was greatly enlarged, and became the " Worcester House ;" and the spacious yard in front, cleared of its trees and shrubbery, has been filled with an elegant four story block.†

The Worcester House ground has historic associations much older than those to which I have referred. Before the War of the Revolution broke out, there was a Mrs. Sterne kept a small public house on the spot, in front of which was the usual tavern sign post, on

*The present Church of the Unity opposite the Public Library.
†The Lincoln House Block.

12

which swung a sign bearing the emblems of royalty, and giving to the house its name of the "King's Arms." It was at this house that the tories of the town were accustomed to meet, and lament over the "terrific radicalism" that not only spoke disrespectfully of royalty, but even perpetrated the "great outrage" of destroying a large quantity of tea which the East India Company had sent to Boston for sale, because the government thought it expedient to put a three penny tax upon it for the purposes of revenue. In the meantime the patriots had an association which they called the "American Political Society," which, being in opposition to the government, met and acted secretly at the "Hancock Arms," near Lincoln Square.

My father related to me as one of his early recollections the strange occurrences that happened in Worcester the year before the opening of the war. They grew out of a controversy between the general court and the judges of the supreme court. That court at that time—I think it was in 1774—was composed of five judges, viz., Chief Justice Peter Oliver, and Associate Justices Trowbridge, Hutchinson, Ropes, and Cushing. The general court resolved that

any judge should be considered an enemy of the
country who should consent to receive a salary from
the crown without a grant from the general court.
The associate justices signified their assent to the
wishes of the general court : but Judge Oliver flung
the gauntlet at them. The patriots therefore resolved
that he should hold no more courts, and the jurors
refused to take their oaths before him. The tories of
the town were alarmed. and they got up a petition to
the selectmen to call a meeting of the citizens, to
consider what would be the consequences of the
course that was being taken towards the government,
its judges and other officers. The meeting was held
on the 20th of June, and was addressed by the celebrated tory. Col. James Putnam, who at that time was
one of the most distinguished lawyers and advocates
in the country, and was obliged not long afterwards
to fly to Boston, and subsequently to New Brunswick,
where, history says, he lived and died a colonial judge.
There were undoubtedly some splendid men among
the tory refugees. A protest was offered to the meeting against the proceedings of the patriot party. It
was ultra in its doctrines and denunciations, and the
town refused to receive it. About one in five only of

the voters had signed it ; but having a tory clerk in the
person of High Sheriff Clark Chandler, the protest-
ants were so lucky as to have their rejected protest
entered on the records, and sent to Boston and
published. " The town was in a blaze," my father
said, " when the trick was discovered." A meeting
was at once warned for the 22d of August. It was
fully attended ; and a committee was appointed to
consider what should be done, and report at an
adjournment two days afterwards. At the adjourned
meeting the committee reported that the clerk be
required to expunge, erase, blot out, and forever
obliterate the obnoxious record ; and they made him
do it, not only with his pen, but by dipping his finger
in the ink, and rubbing it all over the recorded protest
in the face and eyes of the whole meeting. They also
required him to make an acknowledgment of wrong-
doing before the town. The signers of the protest
were also required to make a recantation. The patriot
party proceeded with boldness, and called on their
brethren in other towns to assemble here, and aid in
putting down the tory spirit. On the day of the town
meeting, companies marched in from the country
about to the number of between two and three thou-

sand. Timothy Paine, Esq., (of whom I may have occasion to speak hereafter), had just been appointed one of the mandamus councillors of the royal governor; and one purpose of the gathering forces was to compel him to resign the office, and refuse to perform its duties. They sent a committee to Mr. Paine, who very readily complied with their demand, and gave them a writing to that effect. Most of the men who had signed the protest were in session at the same time at the " King's Arms," where they drew up and signed a recantation. But our forefathers did nothing by halves. The troops were paraded in two lines in Main street, extending from the Court House to the Old South Church; and the recanting signers of the protest against the revolutionary spirit and movements were taken from the tavern, and with Mr. Paine were marched through the open ranks from one end of the street to the other. and compelled to stop every few rods, and listen to the reading of the documents they had signed. Such was one scene in life's great drama, as enacted in Worcester at the distance of eighty-one years in the past, at the season of the year when as now there is a pause in the work of the husbandman between the earlier and the later harvests.

A few of the tory recusants refused to sign any retraction ; and I doubt not they were honest in the view they took of the condition of public affairs, and of the impolicy and inexpediency of the great experiment in which the people were about to engage—that of throwing off allegiance to the British crown, and establishing the nationality of the American people. For their timidity I can find a rational apology in the fact that Great Britain was then powerfully strong, and the colonists were weak ; three millions only where the people now number twenty-five millions, and feeble in resources for sustaining their defences against the royal government and its forces. I am not surprised at their conservatism, nor at their reluctance longer to expose themselves to the imminent risks that were sure to come from the struggles of revolution. All men are not equally bold ; and averse to assuming the hazards of war, they sought quiet and security by abandoning their homes, and placing themselves under the protection of the crown in its more loyal colonies.

Yours,

CARL.

CHAPTER XXV

Mr. Editor : — In my last chapter I spoke of the opening of Elm street, through the hay and corn fields where have since been cut other streets, on which numerous tasteful residences have been erected, surrounded with yards and gardens, and ornamented with trees, shrubs and flowers. On the south side of Elm street, fronting on Main, there was a block of land, which is now covered by the Butman and the Warren blocks, and on which, at that time, stood a two story wooden house occupied by the Hon. Calvin Willard, then the courteous and efficient sheriff of the county. That house was removed, shortly afterwards to Pearl street, and has since changed its locality a second time to the corner of Main and Myrtle streets.

That house is one of the historical points of Worcester. It was. as my father informed me at the time, the residence, for many years, of the Hon. Joseph Allen, father of Hon. Charles Allen, Samuel Allen, Esq., and Rev. George Allen, all now residents of Worcester.

The records of Worcester are not very prolific with the name of Allen. There was a Rev. Benjamin Allen, who came from Sudbury with the party from that and neighboring towns who made the first permanent settlement here. If I have not already so written, I will write it now, that two companies had previously made the attempt to settle the place, and failed to do so. This Rev. Benjamin Allen does not appear to have been a man of mark in the community. A grant of land was made to him as a settler in that part of the town which lies around the south end, or outlet, of Quinsigamond lake; and so far as I can discover he lived and died in the quiet, peaceful, and independent position of a tiller of the earth. I mention him only because he was the first inhabitant of Worcester who bore the name of Allen.

Hon. Joseph Allen was undoubtedly of a different family. My father was accustomed to speak of him as though he knew him well, had been intimate with him, and held him in the highest esteem. I remember

that he said that his mother was a sister of Samuel
Adams, the celebrated patriot of revolutionary times ;
for whose head, as one of the Boston rebels, the
British governor of the colony offered a reward : and
that his father—if I do not misremember—was a
highly respectable merchant of Boston, whose name
was James Allen. As a professional man, Joseph
would have attained a high rank in the times in which
he lived : but after receiving the best English and
classical education which could be obtained in the
Boston schools—and they were then the best in the
country—he turned his attention to mercantile pursuits.
From his subsequent life, I have no doubt he caught
the revolutionary spirit from his uncle Sam. Adams,
who was probably a frequent visitor at his father's
house : for it is known that some half a dozen years
before the Declaration of Independence was written,
just after he had attained his majority, he took a stock
of goods from Boston, and opened a general store in
our adjoining town of Leicester : and that he was
intimate and active with Col. Henshaw, and the other
patriot citizens of that town, in all those measures in
which the New England towns engaged with so much
earnestness for a period of a few years antecedent to

and during the Revolution. I remember a remark of
my father, that "Joseph Allen was not born to be a
shopkeeper;" that with the ability, he had the taste,
the education, the acquirements, for a different position in life : and the people appeared to entertain the
same opinion, for when the elder Levi Lincoln was
appointed Judge of Probate, about a year after the
war commenced, and gave up the office of clerk of
the courts, which he had held for a year or two, young
Joseph Allen was considered sufficiently prominent
to be taken from his store in Leicester, and made his
successor in the office. For the long period of about
a third of a century, Mr. Allen continued to discharge
the duties of clerk of the courts; and it was the
remark of my father that even then the people were
very strongly opposed to his giving up the position.
I suppose, from that fact, that the doctrine of rotation
had not even then become a fundamental principle of
political action, and that office-seeking, was not then,
as it now is, a vicious propensity in public men.

I said that the Allen house, standing where Butman Block now stands, with a yard in front, as was
the custom of the times, was historical. It was on the
first Monday in September, 1786,—69 years ago this

month,—that sentries paced Main street back and forth in front of that house, to give warning of approaching danger. It was a day of wild commotion; the day of the Shays Rebellion, an account of which as related to me by my father, I have already given. He saw the sentinels. He saw the Shays men as they marched into town, through Salisbury street, and took possession of the court house, and made their headquarters at the "Hancock Arms." He saw the judges of the court of common pleas and of the sessions, as they came out of Clerk Allen's house, on that black Monday, with General Judge Ward in front, accompanied by the clerk, sheriff and his deputies, and the other officers of the court; and he saw them move with stern and resolute step through Main street to the court house. He saw them met at the door by Capt. Wheeler, of Hubbardston, and Capt. Smith of Barre, who ordered the soldiers under their command, who filled and surrounded the court house, to charge bayonets upon the court and its officers. He saw the glittering steel thrust through their clothes and pressed hard upon their naked bosoms. He saw the brave old chief justice, who had seen too much of the perils of war to retreat before such an enemy, stand as unmoved as a granite rock, and denounce perdition to all who thus opposed the progress of the tribunals of justice. He heard him, for more than an hour, address the soldiers and the great crowd of people that stood about, with the bayonets pressing upon him, in tones of earnest and indignant remonstrance, until the courage of the captains oozed out at their fingers' ends, and their bayonets were withdrawn; when Judge Ward adjourned the court to the "United States Arms" tavern—afterwards, for a long time, the "Exchange Coffee House," and thus close the work of one dark day.

My father once remarked that it was hard for him not to sympathize with the Shays men, for they were prodigiously oppressed by the action of the courts, in piling writs upon writs, and judgments upon judgments, which had to be answered by forced sales of property, at a time when the prices were at a great depreciation as the effect of the eight years' war.

Mr. Allen served his fellow citizens in other capacities than that of clerk of the courts. He was one of three delegates chosen in 1779 to the convention to frame the constitution of Massachusetts: the

elder Lincoln, and farmer David Bigelow being the
other two.   He was also town clerk for at least one
year, and a member of the board of selectmen ; and
as an active whig co-operated with the revolutionary
committees in their correspondence and addresses, and
resolves, and in all their measures for carrying forward
the war.   In later days he was a member of congress
for one term ; and for several years, of the State
council.

Having experienced the benefits of an early education, Mr. Allen was early engaged in promoting the
cause of popular education.   He was one of the
company, spoken of in a former chapter, that built
the old Centre School House as an institution of
learning above the grade of the common schools ; and
ever retaining a deep interest in the town where he
first made a residence in the country, he engaged in
laying the foundations of that excellent seminary, the
Leicester Academy ; of which for a long time he was
the faithful and efficient treasurer : keeping the moneys
with the most scrupulous exactness. and with that
high sense of mercantile honor which was so peculiar
to former generations of merchants.   He was also
united with others in organizing the Second Parish in

Worcester, of which through life he was an earnest and useful member.   He retained his early habits of study and reading to the close of his life ; and it was the remark of all his acquaintances, that beside being one of the most upright of men in all the relations of society, he was the most courteous and urbane of all the gentlemen of his day, and too generous in his sentiments and feelings to be a mere accumulator of wealth.

Yours,

CARL.

CHAPTER XXVI

Mr. Editor: — While we 'were in front of the Allen house my father pointed to a house opposite, on the east side of Main street, at the corner of Mechanic street: and remarked: "That is the Denny house; where lived and died my friend Austin Denny." Of him I have spoken in a former chapter. He had a brother Daniel, who is one of the most respected merchants in Boston; and their father's name was Daniel, who more than half a century ago set up the business of manufacturing cards in Worcester. The house was vacated not many years after the time of which I am writing; and was converted to the purposes of trade. It took fire one night, and was totally destroyed, with two or three small buildings that stood north of it. A larger building was then erected upon the same ground; and three or four years afterwards, in a calm and beautiful night, that was burned also.

On the opposite corner of Mechanic street, stood a low one story building, recently removed, which was then occupied as a "stage office;" and where more stage business was at that time transacted than at almost any other place in the state out of Boston. And next to it was the "United States Hotel;" then the principal public house in the town, and kept in a superior manner, for those days, by the late James Worthington, and afterwards by Worthington & Clark. It was on this spot, my father remarked, that the first tavern was opened in Worcester, by a man by the name of Moses Rice, who came here for that purpose shortly after the third company of settlers had effected a permanent settlement of the place. He said further, that it was the only tavern within a circle of twelve miles; and although the travellers were not numerous, yet landlord Rice was supposed to have prospered well, with such support as he received from the public and the settlers. In the progress of time the little inn by the wayside gave way to a new and larger house, from a sign post in front of which blazoned forth the emblem of its name, the "Sun Tavern." It was at this public house that Judge Ward opened his court on the first Monday in December, 1786; it being an adjournment from the preceding September. That adjournment took place at the "United States Arms," after the scene at the court house, spoken of in my last chapter. It is said to have been the purpose of the court to meet at the house where the adjournment took place; but when the first Monday in December came, the Shays men took possession of the "United States Arms;" and thus compelled the court to open its term at the "Sun Tavern." No business, however, was transacted on that day; and the court adjourned to January, to give the governor time to send troops enough into town from Suffolk, Middlesex and Hampshire counties, to sustain the tribunals of justice, and quench the fires of rebellion.

I do not, at this late day, remember whether my father told me, or not, what became of the "Sun Tavern;" but I remember he said that the "United States Hotel" was erected by our townsman, Mr. William Hovey.

Since the above was written, Mr. Hovey has deceased. He was a man of far more than ordinary powers of mind, and of mechanical genius; and, in his earlier days, of energy and enterprize. Besides

13

the " United States Hotel," he erected other buildings
which were of better character than the architecture of
Worcester had previously been.   I think that it was
the remark of my father that among the houses which
Mr. Hovey built was the double brick one on what
was once called " Nobility Hill," the west side of
Main street, opposite the southwest corner of the
public common ; and the handsome house which for a
long time was the residence of Rejoice Newton, Esq.
on Front street, next east of the Norwich and Worcester Railroad.

After the erection of the Worcester House, and the
American Temperance House, the " United States
Hotel" began to decline.   It passed through various
stages in the process of dilapidation, as a public house,
until, like a broken merchant, it shifted its position to
a second-class street, and now stands — for what purpose I can better guess than tell — upon Mechanic
street, a little west of the railroad ; and where nearly
one hundred and forty years ago, Moses Rice opened
the first inn between Marlborough and Brookfield, for
the accommodation of travellers between the settlement of Springfield on the Connecticut river and
Boston, and where the " Sun Tavern" was afterwards

built, was last year erected a splendid four story
block,* by William C. Clark ; which, in the comparison with the early wayside inn, marks the progress
the community has made in wealth, in thrift and
in the cultivation of the arts of peace.

Mechanic street, which runs from Main street
eastwardly, is an old road, though not as old as Front
street.   It is supposed that the public common, which
was originally much larger than it now is, came well
nigh to Mechanic street.   That street, as appears of
record, is now nearly seventy years old, having been
opened as long ago as 1787 : but for what reason, I
know not, unless that after the ancient burial ground
upon the east side of the common had become so
much occupied by the graves of the early settlers and
their descendants, that the town then took up a lot on
Mechanic street, and a road was opened to it from
Main street.   There were buildings of ancient appearance standing upon it as long ago as I remember
anything in the topography of Worcester.   It is within
my recollection that the meadow once came quite up
to Mechanic street at one or two points : and I often
heard my father say that there was once a dam, built

_____
*Now called the Walker Building.

by beavers, near where the railroad bridge now
stands ; and that in his younger days it used to be
excellent skating every year, in the winter season,
over a large proportion of the ground between Main
street on the west, Summer street on the east, Mechanic street on the south and School street on the
north ; or, rather, perhaps, as far up as the dam of
the " Corduroy Factory"— now the site of the School
street mills ; ground which, twenty years ago, was
in part the basin of the Blackstone canal ; but which
is now mostly covered with houses and mechanics'
shops ; and on which, in June 1854, mechanical property was destroyed, in one single fire, of the value of
at least $300,000.   The beavers perished long since ;
their old foes, the Nipmuck Indians, are almost in
oblivion ; the skaters are gone ; the devastating flames
were scarcely quenched before the wand of " the Industry of freedom" was waved over the ashes, and
other and more substantial edifices have arisen, that
are already the busy hives of industrious, intelligent
and skillful mechanics ; the innumerable products of
whose ingenuity, skill and mechanical precision, in all
the forms in which the various woods and metals are
wrought, are daily sent forth to all parts of the country

where the earth is tilled, the waterfall turns the busy
wheel, the steam engine elaborates power from fire
and water, or civilization avails itself of the conveniences and comforts which the mechanic arts afford.

Yours,

CARL.

CHAPTER XXVII.

Mr. Editor:—On the west side of Main street, a little farther south than the United States Hotel, stood the house which had long been occupied by the Hon. Nathaniel Paine; and beyond the house, on the corner of Pleasant street, was a small, one story wooden building, which had been occupied by Mr. Paine when a practising lawyer, and before he assumed the office of Judge of Probate. What became of the little office, I am not able to say; but the house was moved from its foundations years ago, and now stands upon the west side of Salem street. The ground is now covered by the four story brick building known as Paine's block: * and in the rear, where once was the garden, now stands the brick church of the second Baptist Society, and other buildings devoted to various purposes of trade. There is nothing there now to remind

_____

*Now owned by T. M. Rogers, and the Woodward and Kinnicutt heirs.

me of the quiet old mansion of Judge Paine, as it was when my boy eyes first surveyed it.

My father said that the Paines were an old family in Worcester; that they came here, in the early days of the town, from the point of land that projects down south of Seekonk plains, and makes a dividing point between the waters of Narragansett and Mount Hope Bays; where the town of Bristol now stands. As long ago as 1709, as appears from the Massachusetts records, the grandfather of the late Judge Paine, (Nathaniel, of Bristol,) had his attention directed to the "chestnut lands" upon the west side of Quinsigamond Lake. It happened in this way. Joseph Sawyer and others, petitioned the general court to survey and grant them the lands upon the west side of the lake, that they might make another effort to establish a settlement here. The Council granted the request, and ordered the appointment of commissioners to carry into effect the prayer of the petitioners. Nathaniel Paine, of Bristol, was named in the order as one of the commissioners. But the order was lost in the house. I cannot assert it as a fact, and I cannot now ascertain the truth of it, but it is now my impression that Nathaniel, of Bristol, was early a proprietor

of the land now known as the Paine estate in the
upper part of Lincoln street; and that he may have
come into possession of it by purchase from Nathaniel
Henchman, who owned what was afterwards the Lincoln farm, and whose house, if I remember the spot
where my father said it stood, was in the Lincoln
garden, a little east of the old or original road, travelled between Boston and Springfield, which then
run along by the side of Lincoln Pond, and across the
land which is now known as "Hamilton Square."
It must have been, however, nearly twenty years after
the first permanent settlement in Worcester, that
Nathaniel, of Bristol, occupied the Paine estate; for
his son Timothy, (the father of the late Judge of Probate,) was but a lad, not then in his teens, when he
became a resident in Worcester. He was a young
man of promise, and was early sent to the college of
Cambridge, where he graduated at the early age of
eighteen. He was designed for the profession of law;
but at that time the business of making writs and
deeds was carried on by a set of "Caleb Quotems,"
who *dickered* in other things beside the law, and
impaired the prospect for a young man whose purpose
it was to obtain a living by his profession. It was

about the same time also that the afterwards celebrated
James Putnam came into town from Salem, and
opened a law office. Young Timothy Paine was
intimate with him and profited much from his friendship. Having the offer of the place of clerk of the
courts he accepted the office, the duties of which he
discharged for a period of twenty-four years, until the
suspension of the administration of justice in 1774.
For a period of ten years, he also performed the duties
of register of probate, and likewise of register of deeds ;
and for quite a number of years he was also one of the
selectmen and town clerk. I mention these facts to
show the estimation in which Timothy Paine was
held by his fellow citizens of the town and county ;
and as evidence that he was then a man of mark in
the community. You remember that I gave some
account, in a former chapter, of his having received
the appointment of Mandamus Councillor to the royal
governor ; and of the mode and manner in which he
was induced to resign it, by the interference of the
patriot party, backed up by the three thousand armed
men who came into town to compel the tories to take
back their protest against the patriot cause. Mr.
Paine appears to have borne himself in a dignified

and honorable manner on that trying occasion; and
that he retained the confidence and esteem of his
townsmen, is manifest from the fact that while the
war was in progress, as appears on record, he was
appointed chairman of a committee of the town to
protest, to the legislature, against the imposition of
taxes for the support of government, upon spirituous
liquors, teas, and other articles; and that when the
revolution had gone by, the animosities of parties had
subsided, and civil freedom was assuming the form
and the strength of well-regulated constitutional liberty,
he represented the town for two years in the general
court.

My father said that Timothy Paine had three sons;
all of whom he knew. Their names were William,
Samuel, and Nathaniel; and that he had the ability
to give them a good education, is apparent from the
fact that they all graduated at Harvard College in a
period of seven years. The oldest was William, of
whom I have spoken in a former chapter. He was
born about the time that his father was appointed
clerk of the courts, and was a pupil of the elder Adams
while he was living here as a law student in James
Putnam's office. After leaving college he studied

medicine in Salem, with that celebrated medical practitioner, Dr. Holyoke, whom my father said that he once saw walking the streets of that city, when his head had been frosted with a century of winters. He was one of the signers of the Protest, already spoken of, and for that reason was obliged to take up his residence as a refugee in a foreign land. But as he came back and lived many years on the ancestral estate, it is manifest that political sins, even in those days, were not of that class which a good life can not wipe out. The funeral of Dr. Paine, as it moved from his residence on the afternoon of a spring day, something more than twenty years ago, is among the recollections of my early days. The estate is still owned and occupied by the Paine family, of the third and fourth generations in descent from Nathaniel, of Bristol.

Samuel, the second son of Timothy Paine, who is recorded as a graduate of Harvard College in 1771 —three years after. William, and four years before Nathaniel—assisted his father in his office of clerk and register, and became involved as one of the signers of the Protest. He went to the provinces, and found employment and support in the British service until after the war was over.

The third son of Timothy, was the late Nathaniel Paine, whose residence I have pointed out in the opening of this chapter. He was well known to the people of Worcester and of the county, having filled the office of Judge of Probate for more than a third of a century. I remember his person as he appeared in the probate court, with the venerable Theophilus Wheeler for his register, on one occasion when my father said to me: " Come, Carl go with me, and I will show you the probate court, where the estates of dead men are settled up, and disposed of according to law!" But I have no knowledge of Judge Paine that would enable me to present anything like a truthful analysis of his character; though I remember that an accident, which is too personal in its nature to be here related, once threw me in his way; and that he was pleased to compliment me to my face, for an act I performed, in a manner that satisfied me, at least, that he was a man of excellent discernment, of a high sense of right, and of much native goodness of heart; the worthy son of a worthy sire.

Yours,

CARL.

CHAPTER XXVIII

Mr. Editor:—Opposite the residence of Judge Paine, and on the corner of Main and Front streets, stood twenty years ago, as it did years afterwards, a long, low building known as "The Old Compound." What it derived its name from, I have not been able to discover. When William Harrington, Esq., built his four-story block up on the site, the "Old Compound" was shoved off its ancient foundations; and now, somewhat modernized, it stands on the north side of Pleasant street, on land which was once a part of Judge Paine's garden.* Upon the sidewalk, in front of it, we met a tall, slender gentleman, whom my father shook hands with, and addressed, as "Friend Brooks." They spoke of the times when Mr. Brooks kept a store in that building, and dealt out to the good people of the town and vicinity such articles as passed

*This spot is now occupied by the Odd Fellows' Building.

under the general appellation of " Dry Goods and West India Goods and Groceries ;" meaning thereby rum, molasses and sugar, from the West Indies ; teas, spices, and cotton cloths from the East Indies, and chintzes and hardware from England. The Mr. Brooks, addressed by my father, I recognized afterwards as the crier of the courts. If my memory serves me, it was my father's remark that the " Old Compound," or at least some part of it, was built by one of the Chandlers, and was occupied by him as a store some time in the last century. When we passed it, there was a stove shop in the corner ; a barber's shop kept by Mr. Weiss ; and one or two other shops. As one of the ancient points in Main street, I could not pass it in this my history of former days.

My father directed my attention to an antique house, and store near by which stood upon the west side of Main street, south of Pleasant street. In its day, it must have been one of the handsomest residences in Main street ; with its spacious yard and garden ; its trees and shrubbery. It gave place not long afterwards to the three story brick block, erected by Messrs. Merrick & Dowley, who were then extensively engaged here in the boot and leather business ;

and now the old house stands a memorial of a past century, on Blackstone street, east of the branch of the Worcester and Nashua railroad.

"That house," said my father, "was once the residence of John Nazro: a showy man, and withal, somewhat consequential." He said that Mr. Nazro was at one time, before the commencement of the revolution, extensively engaged in the manufacture of potash, and had his buildings for that purpose on the west side of Lincoln street, a little way above the "Hancock Arms." He was accustomed to tell, with much zest, an anecdote of John Nazro. It was after this fashion. Nazro prided himself upon having an excellent garden: and, like all good gardeners of the present day, he could not endure to have it trespassed upon by his neighbor's hens. Among his neighbors there was one, who was always ripe for fun, by the name of Healey, who lived up Pleasant street. Meeting him one day, Nazro in something of a pet, said to him :

"Healey, if you don't keep your hens out of my garden, I'll shoot them ! "

"Shoot just as many as you please, Mr. Nazro : only send them home after you have shot them."

Accordingly every day or two, Healey feasted from a fat hen which had paid the price of her temerity in venturing into Mr. Nazro's cultivated premises. Nazro was excessively mortified at the discovery he at length made, that Healey was not the owner of a single hen; but that they all belonged to a good widow lady who lived the south side of his garden; and as he was a man of gallantry, he rendered her compensation more valuable than apologies. As for Healey, he did not fail to remind Nazro every summer afterwards, to send home the hens he shot. Nazro's garden, considerably shorn of its dimensions, is now, (1855,) in the market at a valuation of about $50,000. I mention this as an evidence of the change that time has made in Main street.

Opposite the Nazro place, on the north-west corner of the public common, stood the Town Hall. It is now a part of the City Hall—having been enlarged to nearly double its former capacity. The original building, as appears from the records, was erected thirty years ago, in 1825. In the basement there was a store and an engine house; on the first floor, the hall used by the town, which was entered by two doors in front, between which was a small room occupied by the selectmen ; and the upper story was divided by a partition, running lengthwise, into two halls ; one of which, the north one, was for public purposes, and the other, the south one, was occupied by the Freemasons. Before the erection of the Town Hall, the town held its meetings in the south meeting house—that having been for a long time the property of the parish, and the town and the parish being substantially the same.

It being the day of the annual cattle show we went into the hall, which was excessively crowded by men and women, youths and maidens, boys and girls, the substantial yeomanry of the town and county, who had come in to see the exhibition, and participate in the festivities of a sort of annual " harvest home." I had never before seen a cattle show ; but have seen too many since, and the public have seen too many, to admit of any particular interest being derived from any description I might give of it. There was one peculiar feature, however, in that exhibition, which I have missed in the exhibitions of late years, and which, I think, constituted a very appropriate part of the show. It was the multitude of products, that were on exhibition, of female handicraft, ingenuity,

14

and taste, in the shape of needlework, spun and woven work, and things useful and things ornamental, which excited the emulation of the ladies, and made the show a brighter and merrier affair than it has been since that most important and useful branch of the annual exhibition was given up by the society.

I have seen the statement, and probably it is correct, that the land for the common was originally given to the town for the purposes of a common, the church, a school house, and a training field. At the time of which I am speaking it was not fenced in, except the ancient burial ground on the east side. It was traversed by two roads—one running from the north-west to the south-east corners, and the other from the south-west to the north-east corners. Near the centre, stood the hearse house, and also the gun house of that formidable military organization, the Worcester Artillery, commanded by that veteran, Capt. Joseph Avery, who now enjoys the "blushing honors," then won in service, in his rural retreat near the borders of the town of Holden.

I remember that there was a hot discussion about infringing upon somebody's rights, when the town, years afterwards, voted to enclose the common with a fence; and compel people to ride around it; instead of across it; as also when permission was given for a portion of it to be occupied by that nuisance, the Norwich railroad track.

In its day, when the town was much smaller than it now is, the public common answered well the purposes for which it was originally designed. But the city, as the successor of the ancient town, has outgrown its former conveniences. For cattle shows, and like public exhibitions and occasions, other and larger accommodations had become necessary; and I doubt not that when another twenty years shall have passed by, the public will acknowledge and commend the propriety of the expenditure that has been made for other and more spacious public grounds.

Yours,

CARL.

CHAPTER XXIX

Mr. Editor:—It was stated in the last chapter of this my veritable history of Main street, that the public common was originally given to the town for the purposes of education, the church, and a training field. In the early days of New England the church and the town, the ecclesiastical and civil organizations, were nearly synonymous. The two powers were so closely identified as to be almost one in their exercise.

It was in 1713 that the third settlement—the first permanent one—was made in Worcester. It struggled through many hardships; and even in 1721, when Gershom and Jonas Rice, as a committee of the landed proprietors, applied to the general court, through John Houghton, the representative of Lancaster, for an act of incorporation, they begged of that body to bestow its "serious thoughtfulness for the poor distressed town of Worcester." It was about one hundred and forty years ago that the scattered settlers were accustomed to gather themselves together, of Sunday mornings, each man with his loaded gun, at the log house of Gershom Rice, which stood on the south side of the Hassanamesitt (Grafton) road, on the side of Sagatabscot hill; and there they planted the first church in Worcester. Daniel Heywood, from Concord, and Nathaniel Moore from Sudbury, were the first deacons. After meeting in this way till 1717, the community united in a general contribution of timbers, and erected a log house as a place of worship, on a spot of land near the junction of Green and Franklin streets;* the worshippers crossing Bimelick brook, from one side to the other, where Front street now is, and at the other places, upon trees that had fallen across the water. But even in those rude times, the people prided themselves upon their meeting house: and in 1719 they ventured upon the great work of rearing and completing a frame house, upon

---

*This "first meeting-house" probably never existed; for an entry in the Town Books indicates that the private house of James Rice, which stood near where it is claimed the log structure was built, was used for public worship before the meeting-house on the Common was erected.

the spot now occupied by the "Old South Church," on the west side of the common, and east side of Main street. It was a plain, barn-like building, without steeple, and filled with coarse, rude benches. Every year, some improvements were made upon it; the general court at one time making a small grant for its completion. With the money given by the court, the town made a pulpit, and put in some permanent seats. There arose a controversy, which, as I have reason to believe, lasted as long as the meeting house lasted, upon the manner in which the seats should be occupied. Wealth and family considerations, and especially the amount of taxes paid, were claimed as passports to the best seats in the meeting house; and this gave rise to many heart-burnings and bickerings. Some ten years after the raising of the frame, the house had progressed so far towards a completion, that Capt. Adam Winthrop, one of the Marlborough settlers, who early became a proprietor of lands in the town and was evidently an energetic and liberal man, made the generous donation of a set of pulpit cushions; for which the inhabitants, in town meeting assembled, voted him their thanks; and, I doubt not, if they had had a newspaper, they would have voted its publication, provided—as is frequently done at this day—the printer would do it " free gratis, for nothing," which is susceptible of the free translation, *without expense to anyone but himself.*

In 1739—eight years after the county of Worcester was incorporated—a bell was deemed a necessity for the town and the county ; and the two corporations united in a copartnership, and purchased a bell, which was suspended upon frame work about equal distance from the meeting house and the court house, on or near the lot of land now occupied by the City Hotel. But tradition says that there were disagreements between the parties as to the custody and use of the bell ; and the town then bought out all the interest which the county had in the bell : and proceeded in 1743 to erect a steeple on the church. to which the bell was transferred as soon as it was completed.

In 1763, when the first generation of church members had passed away, and the second had come upon the stage, a larger meeting house was found to be necessary. The present house was then erected. It has been increased in length, and been modified in some particulars, from time to time ; yet in all its essential parts it now stands, upon the same ground occupied by the little church of 1719—a specimen of church architecture ninety-two years ago.

It is not my purpose to give the history of the first parish in Worcester: it would occupy too much of your columns, even if I had the ability to present it: and there would probably be but little to distinguish it from the general history of all similar organizations.

There were contests about ministers, often acrimonious: there was the usual amount of discords among the singers, about the seats they should occupy in the meeting house—who should tune and time the music—and especially about that great innovation, as it was regarded, the giving up of the *deaconing* of each line of the psalm before it was sung.

The first minister ordained here, was the Rev. Andrew Gardner. He orginated in Brookline, near Boston, and had been out of college long enough to have reached what is called the " age of discretion " when he was settled in the ministry. But the story has always been, that he was one of those strangely constituted men who have but little adaptedness for the ministry. He was eccentric in his manners: loved his dog and his gun better than his study, and often chased the deer and other game through the woods that covered the hills and skirted the ponds. The parish was poor; his salary was small; and as the people had no special attachment to their minister, they were dilatory and negligent in making their payments. Probably with the hope of mortifying his parishioners, quite as much as from motives of charity, he one Saturday afternoon took from his feet all the shoes he had, and gave them to a beggar; and the next day walked to church and preached through the day in his stockings. He took his dismission about three years after his ordination; and thus left the ground clear for successors of more becoming deportment.

Among the ministers of the first parish who succeeded Mr. Gardner, were Rev. Isaac Burr, who filled the place for a period of twenty years; Rev. Thaddeus Maccarty, for nearly forty years; and Rev. Dr. Austin, for nearly thirty years. The first sermon I ever heard in that house, was preached by Rev. Rodney A. Miller, several years after his ordination, which took place in 1827.

As we were walking upon the common, my father pointed out to me the house which was for a long time the residence of Rev. Mr. Maccarty, and where

his fourteen children were born. It was an old house
when I saw it, two stories high and two rooms on
the ground of the main building, with a projection in
the rear ; and stood, facing the common, on the south
side of South street—now Park street—on what is
now a vacant lot at the corner of Portland street.

My recollections of the building are faint, as it
was either torn down or moved away not long after I
first saw it.

The Old South Church is historical ; and I should
regret, on that account, any change that should remove
it as one of the religious and civil landmarks of the
town. It was not only the altar where our forefathers
worshipped ; but was also the place where for a long
time the town transacted all its municipal business. It
was there that the town held its meetings, and passed
its resolutions relating to the controversy between the
colonies and the mother country prior to the revolution. It was from one of its porches—my father said
it had three at that time, besides the steeple—that
Isaiah Thomas read the Declaration of 1776 to the
assembled people. And it was there that the town
voted those supplies of men and money that helped
materially in carrying forward the war to its consum-

mation in the peace of 1783.   May it long remain,
as a point within our borders, hallowed by the religious associations of a century and a third of progress
and consecrated by the highest devotions of patriotism !

Yours,

CARL.

CHAPTER XXX.

Mr. Editor:—"That is where tory Jones kept a tavern," said my father; at the same time pointing to a place a little way south of the common.* And he then told me a story about the two spies that came here from the British army in Boston about a month before the battles of Lexington and Concord; and I have found his narrative confirmed by the documents, papers and records of that time. It appears to have been the intention of Gen. Gage to march his army from Concord to Worcester, and thus destroy all the means of the revolutionists for resistance to British authority; and as a preliminary step, he despatched Captain Brown, of the 53d regiment of infantry, and Ensign Berniere, of the 10th, to examine all the roads and streams and bridges, and make a general plan of the route, with an account of all such places, as hills

---

*This tavern stood on Main street, about opposite the entrance to Chatham street.

or passes, where an expedition would be likely to meet with resistance. Accordingly in the month of March, 1775, they laid aside their red coats and cocked hats, dressed themselves in the plain dress of country farmers, and set off for Worcester by the way of Cambridge and Framingham and Shrewsbury. Travelling on foot they arrived at the head of Quinsigamond pond in the afternoon of the second day ; and that was considered by them a pass of so much importance that they stopped there and made a careful sketch of the hills and hollows, which, with other plans drawn by them, were found among the papers of the British officers after the evacuation of Boston. Having completed that sketch they walked on, a distance of four miles, as they marked on the plan of their route, through Lincoln and Main streets, and arrived just at dark at Jones's tavern, south of the common. It was Saturday night. They thought that no one observed them ; but they were not aware that there existed here, at the time, a secret political society, composed of thirty or forty of the patriot citizens of the town, who watched closely every movement of strangers as well as of their own people. It was therefore not possible for two strangers to walk through Main street, at that day, with the military air and gait which they could not lay aside nor wholly conceal, and not be observed by some of the secret association.   They went to tory Jones's tavern ; called for a plain supper and lodgings, and fell into conversation with Jones.   Carefully approaching the subject they discovered that his sympathies were all on their side.   Among other things which he set before them was the proscribed tea ; and as the next day was Sunday, during which no person was allowed to travel, or even walk the streets unless he could give a good reason why he did so, they prudently kept in their chamber, and passed the day in perfecting their sketches, and in writing out a description of the route they had travelled.   In the evening of Sunday they walked out upon the east side of the village, went upon " Chandler Hill," and such other eminences as commanded the village, and sketched their position with reference to each other and the town.   Their plans contemplated a fortification on " Chandler Hill," and camping ground for two regiments.   After making their examinations and plans, they went back to the tavern : and in a short time landlord Jones entered their room, and informed them that two of the tories of the town had called and desired to have an interview with them. Even tory Jones had the common infirmity of landlords: he could not have a distinguished guest in his house, and not communicate the fact to his friends. But the two British spies declined to speak with their outside friends, and told landlord Jones to say to them that they were nothing but two sailors recently from sea, who were travelling into the country, and were not in a fit condition to make the acquaintance of gentlemen. Tory Jones bore the message to his friends, and came back with one from them, the purport of which was that they knew who they were, and what they were here for, and intimating to them that it would be well that they should be cautious about exposing themselves, lest their presence here should subject the tories of Worcester to the same inconvenience and indignity, to which their tory friends of Petersham and other places had been subjected, in being disarmed and deprived of all means of self-defense.

Aware that they were in great danger of being discovered and detained, the two spies bargained for an early breakfast, and also for some roast beef and brandy to carry with them, so that they need not be delayed on the road: and at the first breaking of day,

Monday morning, they took leave of tory Jones and his little tavern. Instead of the usual road to Boston through Main street, they crossed the common, went down Front street, and took the narrow and unfrequented road by the side of Pine meadow and over the hill where is now the deep cut and stone bridge of the Boston railroad; and thence by the coal mine to the head of the pond. Passing through Shrewsbury about sunrise, they were somewhat startled while walking down the Shrewsbury hill, at the approach of a horseman in the rear. As he came up, he bade them good morning, and talked with them a few moments as he walked his horse by their side. The tall, straight form of the horseman, and the inquisitive manner in which his penetrating eye surveyed their persons, excited in them the most painful apprehensions for their own safety. At length he bade them a courteous good morning, and rode off rapidly towards Marlborough. As soon as he was out of sight, they turned off the direct road, and took a cross road that carried them around Marlborough through Framingham; and thus they returned in safety to Gen. Gage in Boston.

That horseman was Col. Timothy Bigelow, of Worcester, whom I have spoken of in a former chap-

ter as "the patriot blacksmith of the revolution,"
during which he commanded the 15th regiment of
Massachusetts troops, which was composed of Worcester county men. At the time of which I am
writing he was a member of the Provincial Congress,
a member of the Committee of Correspondence, and
of the secret political society of the town, and captain
of the minute-men, who held themselves in readiness
to render service to the patriot cause at a moment's
warning. He knew that Sunday night, that those two
strangers were at Jones's tavern; and he knew that
they had left at an early hour that Monday morning,
and the road they had taken; and mounting his horse
he rode after them, and overtook them in Shrewsbury
as I have already related. Confirmed in his suspi-
cions, as to their character and the object for which
they had visited Worcester, he rode on to Marlborough
to confer with the patriot citizens of that town, and
make arrangements for their arrest and examination
on their arrival there. They escaped arrest by turning
off the main road.

It was undoubtedly the intention of Gen. Gage to
march a portion of his army to Worcester as soon as
the spring opened: either to destroy the military

15

stores which were supposed to have been gathered here, or to quarter a part of his forces in the country. But the fatal termination of the expedition to Lexington and Concord rendered necessary a change of his purpose.

This little incident of history, eighty years ago, made the little old Jones tavern, south of the common, a historic point in Worcester. It shows how vigilant the patriots of that day were in watching the signs of the times, and detecting every movement of the British government and its tory friends. Captain Bigelow's minute men were composed of sixty-five privates, one captain, two lieutenants, four sergeants, four corporals, one drummer and two fifers. The town required them to train half a day in each week, allowing them a shilling each day as compensation. But so anxious was Bigelow to perfect his men in drill and discipline, that they had met almost every day for months; and when, on the 19th of April, 1775, the messenger, on a white horse, came riding express into town, with the startling news that the war had begun, Bigelow and his men assembled at the summons of the bell; the Rev. Mr. Maccarty came out of his home south of the common, and there, upon the grass just springing green from the earth, in the centre of the troops, arranged in a hollow square, he prayed for their safe return from the dread conflict of arms in 'which they were about to engage. The prayer ceased; the drum beat; and Bigelow and his men marched for Concord; followed, two hours afterwards, by a second company commanded by Captain Benjamin Flagg. They had arrived in Sudbury, adjoining Concord, before they heard that the British troops had been driven back to Boston. They then quickened their march, and halted not until they had reached Cambridge.

Yours,

CARL.

CHAPTER XXXI.

Mr. Editor: — After viewing the common, the town hall, and whatever of interest the exhibition presented—not omitting the caravan of peddlers—we walked up to what then went by the name of " Nobility Hill."* My father pointed to a large house opposite the common, and informed me that " that was once the residence of one of the Chandlers."† He then showed me the " old Chandler house, " and the splendid farm attached to it ; and gave me a running account of the Chandler family. The farm and house‡ had then passed out of the ownership of the Chandlers, and their descendants, and was owned and occupied by the late Abiel Jaques, Esq.

---

*This Hill extended on the west side of Main street from Park street to a short distance beyond Franklin square. It much resembled Court Hill, except that the bank wall was continuous.

†Where Taylor's granite building now stands. The old Chandler mansion was from 1834 to 1869 the residence of Judge Ira M. Barton and his family.

‡On the site of the Ethan Allen house beyond Wellington street.

No name was more closely and more honorably identified with the history of Worcester, for more than half a century, than that of Chandler. It is found scattered through the records of the town, the county, and the state, from near the time of the first settlement of the town to the revolution, when it lost its prestige in consequence of its possessors having taken the royal side in that great contest of the people for nationality. It was natural, perhaps, that they should be found loyal supporters of the British crown, inasmuch as they had held various important offices in the provincial government, and been honored with its confidence as well as with its patronage.

Among the early settlers of the town of Roxbury, there was a William Chandler who came over from England and purchased an estate there, and was admitted to the rights and privileges of a freeman. But he did not live long to enjoy them. He died, and left his estate to his son, John, who continued to occupy it for a period of forty-five years after the death of his father, when, in 1686, he made up a company from Roxbury and the vicinity, and emigrated to Woodstock, now a part of Connecticut, but at that time, with Mendon, Grafton, Uxbridge, Sutton, and

Sturbridge, a part of our county of Suffolk. He was
evidently a man of mind and of energy of character;
and, in those puritan times, distinguished for his devo-
tion to the church. By him and his associates a
church was formed in Woodstock, and he was designated as one of the deacons—an office in those days of
much greater significance, power and influence than
it now is or has been in later times. The maiden
name of the deaconess was Douglas; and after their
removal to Woodstock, she became the mother of
little John Chandler; whose boyhood was passed in
the wilds of Woodstock, with few advantages for education beyond the teachings he received from his
mother and father. The country was new, and in an
unsettled condition; the Indian tribes, set on by the
French settlers in Canada, made frequent onsets upon
the white settlements; and in this emergency the
government authorized the employment of troops to
guard the frontiers. Young John Chandler had then
reached manhood, and with the bravery of a true
soldier he raised a company of " scouts," and was
commissioned as their commander. He was soon
promoted to the post of major, and his brother made
captain. Worcester, Leicester, and Rutland were

the posts which they mainly occupied and defended. With so much zeal did he serve the government, that he was made a magistrate, in which capacity he exhibited so much ability, capacity, tact, and knowledge of law, that when Worcester county was incorporated, in 1731, the governor appointed John Chandler, of Woodstock, chief justice of the court of common pleas and general sessions, and also the first judge of probate in the county. The first probate court was held in July, in the meeting house : and in the month following, the first term of the common pleas was held also in the meeting house, his honor chief justice Chandler being in attendance for that purpose : and the occasion being considered of sufficient importance to be celebrated with appropriate exercises, a clergyman from Lancaster, by the name of Prentice, preached a sermon, and there were other appropriate exercises. At one time Chandler represented Woodstock in the general court : and he was also a member of the governor's council.

When his honor, chief justice and judge of probate, Chandler, came from Woodstock to open the courts in 1731, he brought with him his son John, and gave him the place of clerk of the courts. And

as it was necessary that the office should be kept in
Worcester, clerk Chandler took up his residence here.
At the same time he received the appointment of first
register of probate for the county. He was also register of the deeds: an office which he could fill without
inconvenience, at a time when the deeds of real estate
to be put upon record were comparatively few in
number. For several years he represented the town
in the general court: and on the death of his father in
1743, he succeeded him as judge of the court of common pleas and judge of probate; and, if I am not
misinformed, he was sheriff of the county at the time
of his death in 1763. His wife was a Gardner, from
New York. And they had a son John and another
by the name of Gardner, who was captain of a company at the time of the French wars; and I believe he
succeeded to the office of sheriff on the death of his
father. The revolution was approaching, and sheriff
Chandler found himself involved in serious difficulties.
In the early part of the year 1774, the sheriff had presented to Gen. Gage a complimentary address from
the tory judges of Worcester, congratulating him on
his appointment as governor of the province. Shortly
afterwards, the British troops in Boston went out on

the Mystic river, and took and carried off a small quantity of military stores : and that set the commonwealth in a blaze. The town committees of correspondence in Worcester county, met in Worcester. and took strong ground against the government. They recommended that all military officers throw up their commissions, and organize an independent militia : and when the time came for the court of common pleas to open its term on the first Monday in September, they found the court house blockaded by an army of six thousand men, assembled on invitation from the convention of committees, because, according to their declaration, parliament had corrupted the administration of justice. In the presence of the soldiers, the judges were compelled to sign a declaration that they would not attempt to perform any of the duties of their office : and thus the court house was closed for a period of more than two years, until the organization of a new government after the declaration of independence in 1776. Having thus disposed of the judges, the convention turned its attention to the sheriff. Sheriff Gardner Chandler was sent for to appear before that body. and there. after some sharp words. he was compelled to sign an acknowledgement of his sorrow that he presented the address to Gen. Gage, and to declare that he would do nothing in contravention to the wishes of the people. But the courts were gone, and the sheriff's occupation was gone with them.

In the same year, the famous protest against the action of the political committees—alluded to in a former chapter—was entered upon the records of the town, by the town clerk, notwithstanding the town refused to adopt it; and when the record became known, those proceedings were had which resulted in a public admonition of the town clerk, and a compulsion of him to obliterate the offensive record by rubbing ink all over it with his finger. That town clerk was Mr. Clark Chandler, who, as I have reason to believe, was a son of sheriff Gardner Chandler. The sheriff had also another son, Gardner L. Chandler, who was educated as a lawyer; but abandoned his profession, and engaged in trade in Boston. The sheriff lived on Main street, opposite the common. Mr. Clark Chandler appears to have found his home an uncomfortable residence after hostilities had actually commenced: and so, as tradition says, he fled to Newport, and sailed from there to Boston; thence to Halifax and Canada. But faring hard wherever he went, he returned home to Worcester, and delivered himself up to the authorities, by whom he was put in prison. His health failed in the jail, and by the intercession of his mother he was discharged from confinement; and permission given him to reside in Lancaster, on condition that he would not pass the boundaries of the town.

When the provincial congress passed its act of 1778, banishing from the country all who had gone over to the enemy, and forbidding their return under the penalty of death, it embraced the names of six residents of Worcester, viz: John, Rufus, and William Chandler, James Putnam, Adam Walker, and William Paine.

I have no means of access to the genealogical tree of the Chandlers; but I believe that the proscribed John was a brother of sheriff Gardner, and the third of the name of John whose names are mingled up with our early history. He was said to be a man of note in the community, and was engaged in trade at the time the revolution commenced. He then left the country and went to England, where his claims for losses were at once allowed by the British government, and at this day help to make up the thousand million dollars of debt which Great Britain owes to her subjects. While in England, he acted as a commissioner of the government to adjust the claims presented by his refugee countrymen. Had he lived until the war was over, he would undoubtedly have been allowed to return home, and regain the respect and esteem he had before in the place of his nativity. But he died in London before peace came.*   Rufus was a lawyer, who had been but a short time at the bar when the courts were suspended : and then he went to London and never came back. William returned after the war, and spent the rest of his days in Worcester. Nathaniel was another of the Chandler family, who was educated in the office of the celebrated James Putnam. He practised law in Petersham until the courts were closed ; and then, taking the tory side of the question, he went to England, where he remained until the war was over. On his return he found all things changed ; and having no heart to resume his profession, he went into trade in Petersham ; and towards the close of his life returned to Worcester, where he died near the commencement of the present century.

_____

*An error. He died in London, Sept. 26, 1800.

Other Chandlers there were, of less notoriety, such as Thomas, and Charles, and Samuel. But the revolution seemed to cast a blight upon the name, from which it never recovered. Respectable they were, as my father informed me; but the very name had become so strongly identified with the toryism of the earlier members of the family, that no one of them ever reached any considerable post of eminence in the community. The ladies of the name I have not felt at liberty to present to the public; and shall trespass no farther upon that delicate ground than to say that one of them, Lucretia, the daughter of the last John, was the wife of the Rev. Dr. Bancroft. Of her I have but little recollection; but she, as my father was wont to remark, had talent, energy, and force of character sufficient for a governor of the commonwealth.

Yours,

CARL.

CHAPTER XXXII.

Mr. Editor:—My tour has reached its conclusion. I have presented, in its several chapters, as near as I have been able, a view of Main street as it appeared to me when I first travelled through it, and had my attention directed to such points as were prominent then, and about which was entwined a bright chain, (blackened in some of its links), of those historic associations which are as valuable to us, as a people, as the wealth that has come down from our ancestors. I have given such facts as have come under my observation during the score of years in which I have busied myself in jotting them down, in moments that were not absorbed by severer tasks. Errors I have undoubtedly made; for all histories are but little better than a series of blunders. Yet it is my hope, that in my details of facts, and in my sketches of character, I have not done positive injustice to any of the individuals who once called this *their* Worcester, as we now call it *ours*. And my object is accomplished if I have succeeded in awakening an attachment, which ought never to die out, for the memories of generations over whose ashes the green grass annually springs, the summer flowers bloom, and the autumn leaves fall: and who in their day, walked these streets as we now walk them; cultivated these hills and valleys as we now cultivate them: bought, and sold, and accumulated wealth, as we now buy, and sell, and accumulate; read newspapers and books, as we now read them; discussed and debated the topics of the day, as we now do; reared houses, and stores, and school houses, and churches, as we now rear them; went up to the sanctuary as the men, and women, and children of to-day go: and passed from earth, when "life's fitful fever" was over, as many now do, and as all must, to be succeeded by the countless generations that in long procession are advancing, to take, to hold, and to deliver up, the Worcester that will be, as the Worcester of the past has been delivered up by those who once held its destinies in their hands.

Time is a great innovator. It makes great changes. An early historian tells us that in the pleasant month of September, one hundred and eighty-one years ago, (in 1674), that philanthropic man and zealous Christian, known as "the apostle to the Indians," the Rev. John Eliot, of Roxbury, visited the territory which is now the city of Worcester, in company with his historian, Mr. Gookin, who had at that time the various tribes of Indians, in Massachusetts, in charge as an agent of the government.

Passing down through the southern portions of the commonwealth, they came into the territory which is now Worcester, through Sutton, after a visit to the Indian tribe at Dudley. They found sagamore John and sagamore Solomon, the chiefs of the Nipmucks, at their residence on Pakachoag hill, where now stands the "College of the Holy Cross." The only white man among them was James Speen; their teacher of Christian doctrine, and of the elements of the white man's learning. The scattered tribe was gathered together; and there, upon the hill, in the open air, canopied by the blue arch of heaven, Eliot preached and prayed, and Speen with his Indian choir sung a psalm. The exercises closed by the opening of a court; in which by authority of the British crown, the two sagamores were constituted the rulers of the tribe.   Among the powers, with which they were invested, was one, which, it would seem ought not to have been necessary in that almost pastoral age ; and that was the power to seize and confiscate all " strong drink " that might be brought among the tribe, to rob them of their wits, and prevent the success of the gospel among them.   In sagamore John's rude house on Pakachoag hill, Eliot wrote a letter to the Nashaway Indians at Lancaster, in which civil power was conferred upon one of the tribe.

But although there where no white settlements here at the time that apostle Eliot made his visit, yet the place had been visited twenty years before by settlers in and around Boston ; for the colony records inform us that at a session of the general court in May, 1657, (one hundred and ninety-eight years ago,) a grant was made to Mr. Increase Nowell, of Charlestown, of a tract of land, of more than three thousand acres lying upon the west side of Quinsigamond Lake. But Nowell died ; and five years after that grant was made, the general court gave another thousand acres, adjoining the Nowell grant, for the relief and per-

16

petual benefit of the church in Malden. Yet there
was no change in the face of the country; and in the
tenth year after the grant to Nowell, the general court
established a commission, to explore the Quinsigamond country, and report upon the practicability of
a settlement being made there. The records say that
the commissioners were Capt. Daniel Gookin, Capt.
Edward Johnson, Samuel Andrew, and Andrew Bel-
char, Esq. They made their report in the autumn of
1668; that the territory contained a good quantity of
" chestnut tree land" and " meadow enough for a
small plantation, or town, of about thirty families."
And they reported farther, that if the Nowell and
Malden grants were added to the ungranted land, so
as to embrace territory of about eight miles square, it
would be sufficient to " supply about sixty families."

Such was the report which the commissioners
made to the general court, just one hundred and
eighty-seven years ago this week, and day, (October,
1668,) the 20th of the month, according to the old
style of keeping time, and the 31st according to the
new. Although two attempts had been made to effect
a settlement here, they both failed; and the face of the
country retained, substantially, its primeval appear-

ance for a period of forty-five years after the commissioners made the report that the land was sufficient for a town of sixty families. Then came, in 1713, in the autumn, the Rices and others, who made the first permanent settlement. Then commenced that history, of men and of things, some sketches of which, I have aimed to present in preceding chapters, by way of illustrating the character and progress of this community in a space of time not quite a century and a half in extent. Its struggles were hard. Its progress was slow : so slow that at the end of half a century, notwithstanding Worcester had been an incorporated town forty-one years, and the shire of the county for thirty-two years, its population had reached only to the number of 1478. And when the colonies threw off their allegiance to Great Britain, in 1776, a census was taken, and the population of the town was but 1925. It went through the revolution, bearing a leading part in furnishing supplies of men and money for the war, and in the subsequent trials and sufferings to close up the war and establish the government upon the constitution of 1789, and its population by the census of 1790, was 2095 only ; but 170 larger than it was fourteen years before, at the opening of the revolution in 1776. At the close of another period of forty years, in 1830, an impulse had been given to the growth of the town by the opening of the Blackstone Canal, and its population then numbered 4172; 1,210 greater than at the preceding census of 1820; and 1595 more than at the census of 1810. Not long after the census of 1830, the power of steam began to develop itself in our midst; though at the time I made my tour there was not a steam engine, of any description, in Worcester; either stationary for the driving of machinery, or locomotive for propelling cars. Now the effects of steam are visible on every side. Then there were no streets west of Main street, except Pleasant and Pearl; and no houses in that quarter of the city, except the few that stood upon those streets. Grove street and the streets around Hamilton Square were then a pasture for cows. There was no street, leading out of Lincoln street, east or west. All east of Summer street, between the old turnpike and the Pine meadow road, with the exception of Prospect street, was pasture and woodland. Green street had scarcely a house upon it; and the plain across which it runs, and on which there are now numerous streets and a heavy population, was a cultivated field, quite down to the water's edge. On the large tract of land between Green street and Main street, south of the common, there were no travelled roads. and no houses except the few that stood upon South. (now Park,) street. Southbridge street, now one of the principal avenues into the city, had not then been opened; upon Main street, between Mower's hill and the village of New Worcester, there stood three or four farm houses; and "Goat Hill," where now stands the spacious Oread Institute, with dwelling houses on every side, and its King street and Queen street in the rear, was then a pasture for sheep and cattle.

Whether the tourist through Main street. twenty. or fifty, or a hundred years hence shall be able to report a continued progress of the city in population, in riches, and in all those intellectual and moral means that are the true wealth of a people, must depend largely upon the liberality in sentiment and in action. the generosity in disposition and in manner, of those who now hold in their hands its substantial interests: and can promote or retard its growth at their pleasure. That growth and that progress depend mainly upon the working classes, who should be allowed to reap liberally the fruits of their own industry.

" Let them not
Be forced to grind the bones out of their arms
For bread, but have some space to think and feel
Like moral and Immortal creatures !"

My task is ended.   My story is told.   I will copy
these lines from a noble poet; and then fling away
my pen.

" Let then what hath been, be.   It boots not here
To palliate misdoings.   'T were less toil
To build Colossus than to hew a hill
Into a statue.   Hail! and farewell all!"

Yours,

CARL.

October 31st, 1855.

www.ingramcontent.com/pod-product-compliance
Lightning Source LLC
Chambersburg PA
CBHW020056030726
47498CB00006B/1813